The Friendly Beasts of Faraday Book 4
by
USA Today **Bestselling Author**
SHANNA HATFIELD

Wings of An Angel
The Friendly Beasts of Faraday Book 4

Copyright © 2018 by Shanna Hatfield

ISBN: 9781790654833

For permission requests, please contact the author, with a subject line of "permission request" at the e-mail address below or through her website.
Shanna Hatfield
shanna@shannahatfield.com
shannahatfield.com

This is a work of fiction. Names, characters, businesses, places, events, and incidents either are the product of the author's imagination or are used in a fictitious manner. Any resemblance to actual persons, living or dead, business establishments, or actual events is purely coincidental.

Cover Design by Rob Foote

To those who let go
and learn to fly…

.

Books by Shanna Hatfield

FICTION

CONTEMPORARY
Love at the 20-Yard Line
Learnin' the Ropes
Rose
Saving Mistletoe
Taste of Tara

Rodeo Romance
The Christmas Cowboy
Wrestlin' Christmas
Capturing Christmas
Barreling Through Christmas
Chasing Christmas
Racing Christmas

Grass Valley Cowboys
The Cowboy's Christmas Plan
The Cowboy's Spring Romance
The Cowboy's Summer Love
The Cowboy's Autumn Fall
The Cowboy's New Heart
The Cowboy's Last Goodbye

Friendly Beasts of Faraday
Scent of Cedar
Tidings of Joy
Boughs of Holly
Wings of An Angel

Welcome to Romance
Blown Into Romance
Sleigh Bells Ring in Romance

Silverton Sweethearts
The Coffee Girl
The Christmas Crusade
Untangling Christmas

Women of Tenacity
A Prelude
Heart of Clay
Country Boy vs. City Girl
Not His Type

HISTORICAL
The Dove

Hardman Holidays
The Christmas Bargain
The Christmas Token
The Christmas Calamity
The Christmas Vow
The Christmas Quandary
The Christmas Confection
The Christmas Melody

Pendleton Petticoats
Dacey	*Lacey*
Aundy	*Bertie*
Caterina	*Millie*
Ilsa	*Dally*
Marnie	*Quinn*

Baker City Brides
Tad's Treasure
Crumpets and Cowpies
Thimbles and Thistles
Corsets and Cuffs
Bobbins and Boots
Lightning and Lawmen

Hearts of the War
Garden of Her Heart
Home of Her Heart
Dream of Her Heart

Chapter One

Drake Miller glanced at the clock on the wall across from his big oak desk and stood as the five-minute bell rang. "It's time to put your things away and get ready to go home," he said, smiling at the fifteen little faces staring up at him in Faraday School's first grade classroom. "Billy's row goes first today."

The students put away pencils and crayons, shoved books and papers into their desks, and then filed to the back of the room in a somewhat orderly fashion due to Drake's diligence in teaching the students over the past three months of classes.

Hooks and shelves were soon emptied of coats and bags.

"Good job, everyone!" Drake praised. The students kept the noise level down and no one got into a shoving match as the children made their way back to their desks with their things.

A tap at the classroom door drew his gaze to the portal as one of the office aides opened it and stuck her head inside. "I have a message for you, Mr. Miller."

"Thanks, Sienna," Drake said, crossing the room and taking the message from the high school student. Aware the sixteen-year-old had a crush on him, he was careful to do nothing to encourage her attentions. Politely, he nodded his head as she backed out of the room, gawking at him with a lovestruck look on her face. He quietly closed the door and opened the message.

After reading it, he tossed it on his desk and turned his gaze to one of his best students, an imp of a boy sitting at the front of the center row of desks. "Nick. Your mom is running late. She'd like you to wait here with me for a few minutes. Okay, buddy?"

Nick nodded and set his coat on top of his desk as though the news was not unexpected.

"All right. Formation time, class! Emily, let's start with your row. Everyone, line up behind her." Drake watched as the students got in line, eager to be released from school for the day.

When the bell rang, Drake opened the

classroom door and bid each student goodbye as they made their way outside to the big yellow buses or to greet parents who awaited them.

He watched to make sure all of his students made it outside where the aide on duty kept an eye on the youngsters.

Assured all was well, he stepped back into his classroom and smiled at Nick. The boy had moved to the carpeted area where Drake read aloud to the students. That corner of the room was surrounded with shelves full of books. A big rocking chair his brother, Drew, had helped him rescue from a roadside garbage pile provided a place for him to sit while the students gathered around him on the soft carpet. It had taken him and Drew two days to scrape off the lime green paint that covered the rocking chair and refinish it, but when they were done, the chair looked great, especially padded with a thick cushion his mom made for the seat.

Nick sat on the carpet with his back against a shelf with a book in his hands. The boy loved to read, but then again, Nick Carol was a bright, inquisitive student who kept Drake on his toes.

If he played favorites, which he absolutely tried to never do, Nick would have been at the top of the list. Drake liked to think his feelings toward the boy had nothing to do with the fact he'd been in love with Nick's mother since she moved to Faraday three years ago. The first time he'd bumped into Angela Carol at the grocery store, he'd felt sharp, breath-stealing pain rip through his chest. He'd known in that moment she'd captured his heart. Unfortunately, the young widow didn't seem to return his feelings or have any romantic inclinations toward him.

Not that he'd worked up the courage to ask her out. He'd stood back and watched her turn down offers for dates from just about every eligible bachelor in town, and a few who weren't. Perhaps because he hadn't asked her out, Angela had gifted him with her friendship. Although he wanted more, so much more, he was grateful to have that much from her.

Angela was a beautiful, smart, successful woman. She'd moved to town and gone into practice with old Doc Johnson who had been Faraday's veterinarian for as long as Drake could remember. When Doc retired a year ago, Angela bought the business and now served as the lone veterinarian in Faraday. She worked long, tiring hours and often took Nick with her on her calls since she had no family in town to help with her son's care.

Drake had even watched Nick a few times when Angela was in a bind. He didn't mind, though. Nick had stolen his heart just as much as Angela had.

"Hey, buddy, want to help me with…" Drake's words trailed off when a loud thump at the window drew his attention.

Nick jumped up and ran over to the window. He stood on tiptoe to look out where a bird had flown into the glass and landed in the landscape bark beneath the window.

"Look, Mr. Miller!" Nick pointed to the bird. "We have to help it!"

"Okay, Nick. Get your coat and let's go see what we can do." Drake snatched his jacket from a hook and grabbed an empty shoebox from the supplies he kept in a tall cupboard near the coat area in the back of the room. He poked a few holes in the top, lined the box with an old towel from a pile of rags he kept in the cupboard, and hurried out of the room.

Nick trailed after him, yanking on his coat and pulling his stocking cap from the pocket to cover his ears.

Together, the two of them rounded the building and hurried over to the outside of Drake's classroom.

"Look, there," Nick said, racing over to where the bird remained motionless between two trimmed boxwood hedges.

"Careful, buddy," Drake cautioned as he knelt by the bird. Gently, he picked it up. Although it looked dead, he could feel the steady beat of its heart. He placed it inside the towel-padded box and set the lid over it. He remembered Angela once telling a client who brought in a wounded bird that it just needed a few hours in the dark to recuperate.

He hoped that would be the case with this bird. In spite of his mother being a vet, Nick struggled with injured animals. The little boy tried to drag home every stray and homeless animal he encountered.

Angela had a dog, two cats, and a sheep because she couldn't find homes for the animals after Nick insisted she help them.

"Is he going to be okay, Mr. Miller?" Nick

asked as they headed back to the classroom.

"I think so, Nick. We'll ask your mom when she gets here." Drake walked inside the room and set the box on a corner of his desk.

He took off his coat and hung it up, then smiled at Nick. "Want to help with chores?"

The boy needed a distraction and Drake was always grateful for assistance with the routine he went through each day once the students left. It wouldn't be the first time he'd set Nick to work after school. Angela couldn't always get away from the vet clinic or make it back from a house call to arrive when school ended for the day. Drake was more than happy to keep an eye on the boy and the times Angela hadn't been able to make it were few and far between, so he knew it wouldn't become a habit.

Nick left his coat on a hook by the door then ran over to the big cupboard where Drake took out a container of disinfectant wipes and handed it to the boy. "Go to town with it, bud."

"These smell like flowers. I like the orange ones best," Nick said as he pulled a wipe from the container and rubbed it over the desk closest to him.

"Smell preference noted," Drake said, taking a handful of wipes to the other side of the room where he scrubbed off desks and chairs. Some might call it paranoid, but he did his best to keep germs to a minimum in his classroom. The daunting task seemed never ending with fifteen first graders, but he did his best. He'd instilled the need to cough and sneeze into their bent elbows, provided gallons of hand sanitizer, and encouraged students to wash their hands when they came in from recess and before eating. Every day after class, he disinfected desks, chairs, equipment, doorknobs, shelves, and even scissor handles and markers. It added a few extra minutes of work to his day, but it was worth it. Since school started in mid-August, the children who'd come to his class sniffling hadn't shared their germs with too many of the other students and he'd remained healthy. Then again, Drake rarely got sick.

"You're doing great, Nick. I sure appreciate your help."

"You're welcome, Mr. Miller." Nick grinned at him as he started down another row of desks, wiping each surface with care. "Do you think my mom will be here soon?"

Drake glanced at the clock. School had been out for nearly half an hour. "I'm sure she'll come as soon as she can. Do you need a snack?"

"Yep! Soon as we finish with this. Do you think Mom would mind if we went to your mom and dad's place to wait for her?"

Drake bit back a grin. One of Nick's favorite places in Faraday was the café Drake's parents owned and operated. His folks spoiled the boy anytime Angela brought him in. A few times when Angela needed a babysitter for an hour, Drake had taken Nick there to wait. His mother stuffed the boy full of warm cookies and cold milk, earning Nick's loyalty for life.

"Tell you what," Drake said, hunkering down by Nick as he wiped off the last desk in the row. "If your mom isn't here by four, I'll send her a text and take you to the café. Deal?"

"Deal!" Nick said, rushing to finish the last desk.

While Drake cleaned the rest of the classroom, Nick straightened books on the bookshelf and wiped the day's lessons off the big whiteboard at the front of the room.

"Mr. Miller?" Nick asked as he washed his hands at the small sink in the back corner of the room.

"What do you need, Nick?" Drake asked as he gathered the papers he'd take home to work on later and stuffed them inside his leather messenger bag.

"Did you know my dad?" The boy stared at him as he wiped his hands on a paper towel then threw the towel in the trash.

Drake shook his head. "I didn't know your dad, Nick. Your mom moved here when you were three."

"Oh, that's right." Nick shrugged as he slowly meandered around the desks, as though he journeyed through an obstacle course. "Mom just talks about you a lot, is all."

Drake perked up at that bit of news. "She does? What does she talk about?"

Another shrug. "Just how you're one of her best friends. She doesn't really have friends here. I think she's always too busy."

"She is busy, but that's because she works really hard so she can take good care of you." Drake hunkered down in front of Nick again and placed a hand on the boy's shoulder. "Your mom has more friends than she realizes. Everyone in the community appreciates her and the help she provides to the animals of Faraday."

"I know, but it's not the same as a good friend, is it?" Nick rubbed a finger alongside his freckled nose and tipped his head to the side, awaiting Drake's response.

"No, I guess it isn't quite the same. You're a pretty smart guy, Nick. You know that?"

The boy giggled. "That's what my mom tells me, and she's the smartest person I know."

Drake couldn't argue with him. Instead, he finished gathering a few things he wanted to take home then pointed to the clock.

"What time is it?"

Nick studied the hands on the clock. "Five more minutes, then we'll go. Right?"

"Absolutely right." Drake ruffled the boy's dark brown hair, a trait he assumed came from Nick's father. The boy resembled his mother in every other aspect, from the shape of his face and chocolate-colored eyes to the sweet way he smiled and the habit of tipping his head to the side when he was thinking about something or teasing someone. If he had blond hair, like Angela, Nick would have looked exactly like her.

Thoughts of Angela's luxurious blond locks and the warmth of her smile made Drake wish, for the millionth time, he could be more than her friend and occasional babysitter. He'd ask his brother or one of their friends for suggestions, but he had a strong idea that they'd just torment him instead of offer any help. In fact, Drake knew Drew would take great pleasure in taunting him since he'd so often done the same to his brother and only sibling.

Drake had no idea how he and Drew could be so different. Drew was always big and brawny while Drake was lean and gangly. Drew was quiet, shy, and reserved around people until he really got to know them. Drake tended to be the life of the party and could talk to anyone, anywhere, about anything. When they were younger, Drake was the one who rushed to the front of the line while Drew preferred to linger at the back.

Countless times, Drake had forced Drew out of his comfort zone, thinking he was helping him, but it only served to push Drew further into his shell. He'd finally learned to leave his brother alone and let him do his own thing. Drew had left home, gone to college, and returned to Faraday to take the position of full-time mail carrier in their small town where there was only one mail route. A couple of women took care of the rural routes and one worked the window at the post office, but they were all older and married.

Drake took a small bit of comfort in the fact his dating life was not any more pathetic than that of his brother or their two good friends, Seth Stafford, a local rancher, and Rhett Riggs, the owner of Faraday's gas station and garage. The two men had gone to school with him and Drew and they'd remained friends over the years.

Seth had never wanted to live anywhere except on the ranch where he'd grown up with his grandfather, Sam. Rhett couldn't shake the dust of Faraday off his feet fast enough after he graduated, but once his uncle's health declined, Rhett came back from Portland to care for eccentric Will Bolton. After all, Uncle Will was the only one in town, perhaps the whole state, who'd owned a camel. Upon his death, Will left everything he owned, including Lolly, their resident celebrity, to Rhett. The camel caused his friend plenty of trouble with her tendency to wander out of her pen.

"Can we go now?" Nick asked, breaking into Drake's musings. The little boy pointed to the clock.

"Okay. Let me text your mom so she knows..."

"Knows what?" Angela Carol asked as she breezed into the classroom.

"Mommy!" Nick shouted and launched himself into her arms.

Angela hugged him close and kissed his cheek before she set him on his feet and drew him back against her with her hands resting across his chest. "Were you good for Mr. Miller?"

"Of course!" Nick looked up at her with a grin that no adult with half a heart could resist.

Angela kissed him on the forehead. "That's my boy." She looked up at Drake and smiled. "Thank you so much for letting him stay. I'm so sorry I was late. Someone's dog got hit on the highway and they brought him in about five minutes before I should have left to pick up Nick."

"It wasn't a problem at all," Drake said, giving her a reassuring look. "Nick's a great helper."

"Mom, come here! You need to help us," Nick said, pulling Angela toward Drake's desk.

Drake stepped over to his desk and placed a hand on top of the shoebox where they'd left the bird.

"A dove hit the window and knocked itself out. Nick and I put it in this box, but I figured you'd know what else to do to help it." Drake slid the box toward her.

Angela slowly lifted the lid just enough to peek inside. "Looks like Mr. Dove is still sleeping. I'll take him with me so I can keep an eye on him." She turned to Nick and cupped his chin in her hand. "Grab your coat, baby. We need to get going. I promised Mrs. Burnside I'd stop by to check on a cat she says is staying on her back porch. She's worried it might be hurt because it walks funny, whatever that means."

"But, Mom, I'm hungry. Can't we go to the café? Please?" Nick retrieved his coat and put it on while he begged.

"I've got dinner cooking, Nick, and snacks in the truck. The sooner we go see Mrs. Burnside, the sooner we can go home." Angela handed Nick his backpack then turned to Drake.

"Thank you, again, for allowing him to stay. I know I shouldn't ask you to do that, but I so appreciate your help, Drake." She stood on tiptoe and kissed his cheek.

Drake stood perfectly still lest he turn his head and make sure the kiss landed on his lips. When Angela moved away from him, he smiled at her, wondering if she could see his heart in his eyes. "You're welcome, Angela. I'm always happy to help when I can."

"I know. That's what makes you such a good friend." She squeezed his hand then turned to Nick, nudging him toward the door. Drake walked beside her carrying the shoebox with the bird. At the door, she took the box from him. "I'll let you know how our feathered friend does later."

Drake knew that meant she didn't want to worry Nick in case the bird died. He walked with them to the outside door and held it open for her. "Sounds great, Angel." *Whoops.* He hadn't meant to call her that, even though she looked like one as she stood in a shaft of late afternoon sunlight. The golden streamers created a soft glow around her, like she wore a glowing halo instead of just her hair twisted back in a messy bun. With her rosy cheeks and perfect ivory complexion, he had no problem at all imagining her as a celestial being.

Afraid of what her reaction to his slip up might be, he bent down and grinned at Nick. "Hey, thanks again for your help, buddy."

"Anytime, Mr. Miller. Bye!"

"Bye, Nick."

Drake waved once then hurried inside, mentally kicking himself all the way back to his classroom. He'd better rein in his thoughts where one gorgeous vet was concerned or he'd end up losing her friendship. For now, friend status was better than nothing at all.

Chapter Two

"I'm really, really sorry I was late picking you up today, baby," Angela said, glancing in the rearview mirror at her son.

Nick munched on celery sticks filled with peanut butter that she'd packed for his afternoon snack. In between bites, he slurped apple juice from a straw poked in a juice pouch. "It's okay, Mom," he said, after he swallowed the bite he was chewing. "I always have fun with Mr. Miller."

"I know you do, honey. He's a good teacher

and a good friend." Angela wouldn't allow herself to think about just how good of a friend the handsome, friendly man had been to her since she moved to town. She certainly wouldn't consider the kind of friend she wished he could be. The door to that type of dreaming was not only firmly closed, but also nailed shut.

Three years ago, she'd been wandering through the grocery store, questioning whether moving to the small town of Faraday had been the right thing to do. She turned at the end of an aisle and collided with an attractive man who welcomed her to town with an honest, inviting smile.

Drake introduced himself, teased a grin out of Nick, who'd been so young and unsettled by the changes in his life at that time, and endeared himself to her. Her heart had pitter-pattered at the sight of the dimple in his chin and the light that seemed to shine from his warm blue eyes.

If she was willing to allow herself to fall in love again, Drake was the one person capable of winning her heart. After all, he'd called her Angel today. No one called her Angel, not ever. But she'd certainly liked the way it sounded when he said it. Under other circumstances, before her life had so drastically changed, she would have thrown herself at Drake's feet and begged him to love her.

Unfortunately, her heart was safely encased behind a thick, impenetrable wall she'd erected before her husband died, and she had no plans to ever go down the road of matrimony again. But if someone could master the impossible and entice her in that direction, Drake was the man for the job.

Tall and lean with a head full of brown hair, Drake was outgoing, funny, sweet, goofy, and, in her estimation, one of the nicest guys on the planet. She had yet to meet anyone in the Faraday community who had a bad thing to say about him. Drake always seemed engaging, intelligent, patient, and supportive, not to mention strong. She'd seen the way he easily picked up Nick and swung him around as though he weighed no more than a bag of feathers.

Everyone at Faraday School raved about him, not only because his students were well-behaved and eager to learn, but also because he was *that* guy who made everything seem more fun, special, and exciting. She knew he was often among the first to arrive at school in the morning and the last to leave. If one of the other teachers needed help, he was quick to lend a hand. She'd even seen him filling in as a temporary coach with the junior varsity basketball team one afternoon when the regular coach was out sick.

From past conversations with Drake, she knew he could have been a pro basketball player. He'd been on track to make it to the NBA when he sustained a career-ending injury during his junior year of college. Unable to pursue his dream career, he switched gears and went into teaching.

It surprised her that he'd chosen to teach first-graders when he could have been a high school teacher and coach. When she questioned his choice, he told her he possessed the energy and stamina needed for the younger grades. He wanted to be able to share his enthusiasm for life and learning with them when they were still young and so very impressionable.

Drake was an amazing teacher and Nick clearly loved him. Truthfully, Drake was one of the few people in town she trusted to watch over her son. Not that she couldn't trust others, she just hadn't invested the time in friendships that a deeper level of trust required. However, she knew Drake well along with his brother, Drew, and their parents.

She'd met a newcomer to town a few months ago, Joy Cooke, when a donkey showed up in the woman's backyard. Pete, as Joy named the donkey, had obviously suffered from abuse. Joy called Angela to treat the donkey for his injuries and the two of them spent a while chatting. If Angela had time to work on building friendships, Joy would be among those she sought out.

Nevertheless, she had no close female friends. No girlfriends to shop with or tell secrets to, or dish with about guys. Angela didn't have time for things she currently considered frivolous, even if there were activities and pastimes she used to enjoy and now missed. It had been years since she'd gone to a mall and wandered through the stores just for fun. The last time she'd done so seemed like a lifetime ago, when she was a completely different person. One who still believed in fairytales and finding her very own prince charming.

Right now, her little boy was her entire world and she'd do anything to protect him. Anything.

"Is Mr. Dove still being quiet, baby?" Angela asked as she turned down a side street and drove to a house that had been painted a glaring shade of purple. Poor Mrs. Burnside refused to admit she was nearly blind, but the only one she fooled was herself. People cleared out of her way when she drove through town and did their best to help her when she shopped because she could no longer distinguish colors or labels. Obviously, the paint counter at the hardware store hadn't gotten the memo about helping Mrs. Burnside with her color selections.

"I think he's still sleeping, Mom. Should I wake him up?" Nick asked reaching for the shoebox on the seat next to him.

"No, let him sleep for now. I'll leave the engine running so he doesn't get cold. Do you want to stay in the truck or come with me?" Angela asked as she picked up the medical bag she carried with a variety of supplies, uncertain of what she'd find with Mrs. Burnside's stray cat.

"I'll come with you, Mom. You might need my help," Nick said, unfastening his seatbelt and climbing off his booster seat. He opened the back door and jumped down from the pickup before her feet touched the ground.

Angela took his hand in hers as they made their way up the front walk. Nick stared at the gaudy purple paint and started to say something, but she shook her head and made a locking motion with her fingers next to her lips, the signal for him to keep his thoughts to himself.

Nick pushed the doorbell and they waited, listening as Mrs. Burnside's footsteps grew louder as she approached the door.

"Who is it?" the old woman asked.

"It's Angela and Nick Carol, Mrs. Burnside. You asked me to check on the stray cat."

"Oh, yes, I did," Mrs. Burnside said, yanking open the door. "Come on in."

Angela darted a glance at Nick and gave him another lock-your-lip signal as they both tried not to gape at Mrs. Burnside's outfit. The long, flowing orange tunic she wore clashed with the pink floral vest that topped it. Bright green pants and fuzzy yellow slippers completed her vibrant outfit.

Uncertain whether the woman dressed that way intentionally or because she couldn't see the colors, Angela had to look away to keep from asking the question.

"The cat is on the back porch. I just fed him a few minutes ago. He acts so strange and makes the oddest sound," Mrs. Burnside said, preceding them down the hall and into the kitchen. She opened the back door and stood to the side. "He should be there by the food bowl."

Angela glanced down at her son. "Stay right here, Nick. If I need help, I'll let you know. Okay?"

"Okay, Mom," Nick said, still distracted by Mrs. Burnside. He studied the woman as though he expected her to put on a clown's wig and perform a magic act or two.

Angela stepped outside and looked to her right, but saw nothing unusual. A growl to her immediate left, though, caused her to slowly turn her head toward the sound while her body remained still. The guttural sound was definitely not from a cat.

"Hear him, dear? That's not normal for a feline, is it?" Mrs. Burnside asked from inside the kitchen.

"No, it isn't." Angela blinked twice. Mrs. Burnside's supposed cat was a huge raccoon, one of the biggest she'd ever seen.

The raccoon hissed and bared his teeth before running toward her, making it clear he wanted no interference with his free meal plan from the sight-impaired old woman.

Angela yelped and raced inside the kitchen, slamming the door before the raccoon could run inside.

"Mommy?" Nick asked, concerned by her scream and the fact she leaned against the door, her breath coming in tight gasps.

"It's okay, baby. There's a raccoon out there, not a cat."

"Oh, gracious!" Mrs. Burnside said, hurrying over to peer out the window by her kitchen table. "Do you suppose it ate the cat?"

"No, Mrs. Burnside, the raccoon did not eat the cat. The animal you've been feeding isn't a cat. It *is* the raccoon."

"Oh, I'm sure you must be mistaken, dear. The cat had a dark face and the cutest little paws, almost like fingers and he makes the most adorable little growling sound when I put out his food. Sometime he stands on his back legs and holds out his paws, like he's begging. He's just precious, but if he's gone that wretched beast must have swallowed him whole!"

Angela rolled her eyes and placed an arm around Nick. "Mrs. Burnside, there is no cat. There never was a cat. Only the raccoon. I'll call someone to come get it. They'll probably be here tomorrow."

Angela nudged Nick forward so they could leave. "Under no circumstances should you open that door tonight. Is that understood?"

"Of course! I don't want that blood-thirsty monster in my house!" Mrs. Burnside pressed a hand to her throat, as though the raccoon held the power to summon unchecked death and destruction if he gained entry to her home.

"Just stay inside, Mrs. Burnside, and everything will be fine," Angela assured the woman as they walked to the front door. "Do you need anything before we leave?"

"No, dear. I'm all set for the evening. Wait until I call Gladys and tell her I've got a masked devil trying to get in my house." Mrs. Burnside's fear quickly transformed to glee. "Why, I bet it'll set the phone lines buzzing all evening, especially if I don't tell them it's a raccoon. I bet Bertha will think it's that weird little man who hangs out at the pool hall."

"Just remember you aren't to open the back door." Angela patted the woman's arm, then took Nick's hand in hers and jogged out to her pickup. Once Nick was fastened into his seat, she turned around and grinned at him. "That was interesting, wasn't it?"

"Oh, Mom! Mrs. Burnside thinks the raccoon is her kitty!" Nick erupted in laughter and giggled all the way home. He was still amused as she drove around the side of their one-story craftsman home and parked in the big garage at the back of the house.

Angela gathered her things then picked up the

box with the bird and led the way into the house. The smell of dinner filled the air with a pleasant aroma that made her stomach growl. She couldn't remember if she ate lunch or not then recalled she'd started to eat her sandwich when she had an emergency call to a farm a few miles outside of town. By the time she returned to the office, she'd seen three furry patients before the distraught owner carried in the dog that had been hit on the road.

Some days she was glad for the hectic, busy pace of her practice. It kept her from having the time or energy to dwell on the complete lack of balance in her life. Other days, she wished she could sleep in, visit a spa, maybe have her nails done, eat a leisurely lunch, and take a nap.

"It'll never happen," she murmured as she set her things down in the laundry room that connected to the garage. She and Nick kicked off their boots. While Nick hung up his coat and carried his backpack into the kitchen, Angela set the shoebox on the dryer and carefully opened the lid. The bird blinked at her, but didn't move. "Hey, Mr. Dove. Looks like you need a little more time to be ready to fly. I'm going to leave you right here and come back in a bit to check on you."

She padded the top of the dryer with a thick towel so it would be warmer for the bird, and set his box on it then removed her coat. She left the rest of her things on a narrow table by the door. Before she left the laundry room, she flicked off the light so the bird could rest.

"Dinner smells good, Mom. I'm starving," Nick said as he balanced on his midsection over the edge of the sink and washed his hands. "What are we eating?"

"One of your favorites. I made a hobo dinner." Angela smiled as Nick jumped down and did a fist pump in the air. Her boy gobbled up anything with meat and potatoes, although he was generally a good eater and not picky. But he loved the meatloaf and sliced potatoes meal she cooked in the slow cooker by wrapping the potatoes in foil to keep them separate from the meatloaf.

With time at a premium, Angela had learned to make a variety of meals she could put in the slow cooker in the morning and come home to enjoy at night. She had it down to an art and could even whip up a dessert in the slow cooker if necessary. Between eating leftovers and the two or three meals she made during the week, she and Nick always had a nice dinner. Thank goodness for the slow-cooker liners she bought by the dozens that made clean-up a breeze.

"You set the table and I'll get everything ready."

Angela was proud of her little boy. For the most part, he rarely fussed or whined, and usually minded. Many times, he jumped in to help her before being asked. While she appreciated him, appreciated his helpfulness, she worried sometimes that he was growing up too fast because it was just the two of them. She couldn't help but wonder if Nick would allow himself to be a carefree kid if he had a father figure at home.

In spite of her worries about her son, she couldn't help but grin as Nick set plates and silverware on the kitchen table while he sang a song Drake had taught the students.

"Guess what, Mom," Nick said as he took a few running steps and slid on his sock feet across the kitchen floor, almost taking a nosedive into the fridge.

Angela caught him before he fell and tickled his sides, making him giggle and squirm. "What, baby?"

"When Mr. Miller asked us to spell words today, I got mine all right and got to pick something out of the treasure chest."

"You did? That's awesome," Angela said, giving Nick a high five. She thought it was brilliant of Drake to keep a wooden chest that really did look like a pirate's chest full of little toys and treats. He randomly used it to reward students for doing well. Nick always got so excited when he was able to choose something from the chest. "What did you pick?"

Nick dug into the front pocket of his jeans and pulled out a small red yo-yo. He held it out for Angela to see.

"Oh, I had one of these when I was a kid. I loved playing with it." Angela turned from the green beans she'd just popped into the microwave to heat and took the yo-yo in her hand. She tied a loop in the end of the string and slid it over her middle finger then gently tossed the toy away from her and pulled it back.

"Yay, Mom! You made it go!" Nick clapped his hands and hopped from one foot to the other. "Can you teach me to do that?"

"Sure, baby. Right after dinner and homework, and feeding the animals." Angela should have stopped long enough to check on their pets when they first arrived home, but she didn't want to leave the dove in the cold and she was as hungry as Nick claimed to be.

"Okay, Mom," Nick said, skipping across the kitchen. He opened the fridge and started to pull out the gallon jug of milk, but Angela grabbed it before he dropped it.

"I think that's still a little heavy for you, son." She broke the seal on the cap and unscrewed the lid. "If the milk jug holds 16 cups of milk…" Angela poured two glasses full and screwed the lid back on. "And we just took away two cups, how many are left in the jug?"

Nick tipped his head to the left and got such a look of concentration on his face, Angela had to tamp down a laugh at his comical expression. She set the glasses on the table then retrieved the green beans from the microwave and set the bowl on the table.

"Is it fourteen?" Nick asked, slightly hesitant with his answer.

"You are such a smart boy, baby. That's exactly right. Good job!" Angela gave him a hug and he beamed with pride.

"Mr. Miller says I'm good with math, but I like reading best." Nick gave her a playful grin. "And recess."

Angela tweaked his nose. "Oh, you!"

He giggled as she sliced the meatloaf and transferred the potatoes to a serving bowl. She set the food on the table, then took a seat. Nick sat beside her and took her hand in his as Angela offered a brief but heartfelt prayer of thanks for the meal.

Nick chattered between bites of food, telling her all about his day. When they finished eating, he carried dishes to the dishwasher and loaded them while she stored leftovers in the fridge.

Without being told what needed to be done, Nick followed her to the laundry room where they both pulled on old coats and muddy boots then headed outside through the door in the side of the garage. While Angela fed the sheep, Nick made sure the cats and dog had food and water.

Angela had installed a little doggie door in the garage so the cats and dog could come and go as they pleased.

"Be nice to the kitties, Brutus," Nick said, petting their three-legged mutt. The dog had been found on the road with a broken leg. Angela had to remove part of it to save the canine, but no one ever showed up to claim him, so she let Nick keep him. The two half-grown cats had been dumped at her clinic one morning and she didn't have the heart to tell Nick he couldn't keep them when he promised to take care of them. He had done a good job keeping Oscar and Grover fed, watered, and lavished with attention, although Angela insisted they could not become house cats.

Their house sat on ten acres behind the vet clinic. The previous vet had built the house about fifteen years ago. The home offered three bedrooms, two bathrooms, a master suite that had become Angela's haven at the end of a long day, and a comfortable, safe place for them to live. When Doc Johnson agreed to sell her the vet clinic, he included the house and acreage in the sale. The man had moved to a small house in town and seemed to be enjoying his retirement.

The location of the house was convenient for Angela to be close to work, and gave Nick plenty of room to run and play in the summer, where she could keep an eye on him from the clinic. A garden shed, three corrals, and two barns sat on the property between the house and the clinic. Angela kept the smaller barn free from clinic patients since it was home to Nick's sheep, Shep.

She'd acquired the curly-horned pet when she'd gone out to a farm to doctor a sheep a coyote had attacked. While she was there, the farmer mentioned a little runt triplet he didn't have time to care for. Angela couldn't bear to see anything happen to the little lamb, so she brought it home and she and Nick raised Shep on a bottle. Half the time, the crazy ram thought he was a dog, following Nick around and obeying his commands.

The rest of the time? Well, she wasn't quite sure what went through Shep's head. Twice in the last few weeks he'd escaped his confines and headed for the road. She had no idea where he planned to go, but wherever it was, he was in a hurry to get there.

While Nick lavished attention on the dog and cats, she stepped inside the house and picked up the shoebox, carrying it outside.

"What are you gonna do with the bird, Mom?"

Nick asked, jogging over.

His breath made frosty puffs in the chilly night air and Angela shivered, ready to go inside, flick on the gas fireplace, and cozy up next to it while she helped Nick with his homework.

"I'm going to take off the lid and see if Mr. Dove wants to fly. If so, he can be on his way. If not, then I'll get a cage for him to stay in until he feels better." Angela removed the lid from the box and handed it to Nick.

The bird lifted his head and watched her, but showed no fear or apprehension. He blinked twice and cooed.

Gently, Angela lifted him from the box and felt along his wings and legs, checking him for any injuries that might prevent him from flying. She couldn't find anything, but the bird didn't seem interested in taking flight. Not at all.

"Why don't you go inside, baby? I'll run over to the clinic and get a cage for Mr. Dove and be right back." Angela tipped her head toward the back door.

"Can I hold him while you get the cage, Mom?" Nick asked, eying the bird.

Angela glanced down at the bird and back to Nick. "Okay, in the laundry room."

They stepped inside and she transferred the bird into Nick's arms. Her son carefully held the dove as he trailed his fingers over its head and down its back.

"If he tries to fly and acts scared, set him down, go in the kitchen and close the laundry room door. Okay?"

"We'll be fine, Mom." Nick gave her a confident look as he continued to tenderly stroke the bird. "Jasper likes it here."

"Jasper?" Angela asked as she opened the back door.

"Mr. Dove said his name is Jasper." Nick tipped his head and bent closer to the dove. "And he said he likes it here."

Angela rolled her eyes. "I'm sure he does. Remember, if he starts to do anything…"

Nick sighed. "I know, Mom. I can do this."

"I'll be right back."

Quickly shutting the door, Angela ran to the clinic, unlocked the back door and found a bird cage that would work for Jasper in the storage room. She grabbed a small bag of feed and hurried home.

When she opened the laundry room door, Nick stood where she'd left him, holding the dove while it cooed softly. The bird's behavior struck her as odd, but she worked quickly to make a place for him to stay. She set the cage on a newspaper-covered card table, lined the bottom of the cage with newspapers, added food and water, then took the bird from Nick.

"Okay, Jasper," Angela said quietly as she set the bird inside the cage. "You just make yourself at home."

The bird hopped onto a perch, tipped his head toward them, and cooed.

"Look, Mom! I think Jasper likes it here." Nick leaned against Angela and she wrapped an arm around him.

"Come on, honey. Let's get out of these old

chore coats and see about doing your homework, then we'll play with that yo-yo you brought home." Angela removed her coat and boots, surprised by how swiftly the temperature had dropped outside. If she believed the old timers she'd heard talking around town, they were in for a long, cold, snowy winter. She sure hoped it waited a while before it arrived. Growing up in Colorado, she was used to snow, but it didn't mean she enjoyed working in it or driving on slick roads.

Nick hastily yanked off his boots and set them on a rubber-lined tray by the door then hung his coat up and raced into the kitchen. After washing his hands, he carried his backpack into the living room.

Angela washed up, made a cup of tea, and joined Nick on the couch after she flicked the switch to turn on the gas fireplace. "Okay, baby. What homework did Mr. Miller give you to work on tonight?"

"I just need to finish reading the story we started yesterday and do five math problems." Nick got out a sheet of paper with math equations printed on it and set it on the coffee table. After he retrieved a pencil from his backpack, he plopped down on the floor and started working on the first problem.

Angela sat back and watched him work, letting him figure out the answers without her assistance. Pride swelled in her chest when Nick answered all five of them correctly.

"You did great, Nick," she said, wrapping an arm around his shoulders and pulling him close enough she could kiss the top of his head when he hopped up on the couch. "Let's finish reading the book."

Nick picked up where they left off the previous evening. The book was fun for a child his age, full of rhyming words that made her son giggle with each turn of the page. When he finished, he snapped the book closed and grinned at her. "That's a good book, isn't it?"

"If it makes you giggle," she poked a finger in his side, drawing out more chortles, "then it must be good."

"Mr. Miller has the best books in his classroom. And he sorts them so it's easy to find ones I like," Nick said, stowing the storybook and his homework back in his bag.

"How does he sort them?" Angela asked as she set down her mug of tea and looked through Nick's bag to make sure there weren't any notes she needed to be aware of.

"He puts all the books with farm animals together and ones with dinosaurs, and books that rhyme, that sort of thing," Nick said, as he jumped off the couch and landed on his feet. He grabbed his bag and took it back to the laundry room so he wouldn't forget it in the morning, then returned to the living room with the yo-yo.

"Teach me, Mom? Please?" He stared up at her with a pleading, rascally grin that she was powerless to deny.

With a feigned beleaguered sigh, she rose to her feet and took Nick's hand in hers, slipping the string of the yo-yo over his middle finger. "The first thing you need to know…"

Chapter Three

Drake parked his SUV in the nearly empty parking lot at the school, grabbed his messenger bag, and headed across the frost-slicked pavement.

He'd been surprised by the thick coat of frost on his windshield that morning. If Sam Stafford's arthritis could be trusted as a predictor of the weather, the old rancher was convinced they were in for an early snow.

As cold air snaked down Drake's neck, he thought Sam might be right. If he'd been fully awake when he left the apartment, he would have grabbed a scarf or at least worn something warmer than a fleece sweatshirt with the school's falcon mascot emblazoned on the chest.

Fingers slightly numb from the cold, he fumbled with his keys and finally inserted the correct one in the lock in a side door and hurried inside. He made sure the door locked behind him before he made his way to the wide hallway of Faraday School.

The main hall, cafeteria, and gymnasium had been built in 1931. A wing was added in 1952 and a second wing in 1964, giving them ample room to educate kindergartners through seniors in high school. The fifth through eighth grades and the school offices were in the wing to the left of the main hall with the high school classrooms in the wing on the right. The main hall was where Drake spent his days, along with the rest of the elementary school teachers.

Overhead lights shone on the polished hardwood floors. Drake wasn't sure, but he thought the floors throughout the building were all original. They'd had excellent care throughout the years.

The aroma of coffee lured him to the cafeteria where three cooks were already busy with the day's preparations. They always made a big pot of coffee for the teachers to enjoy when they arrived in the morning.

"Good morning, lovely ladies," Drake said as he helped himself to a cup of the strong black brew.

He took a sip and dramatically sighed in appreciation. "Now that's good coffee."

"Flattery will get you everywhere, Drake." An older woman with a snowy white bun on her head and the perfect body shape to play Mrs. Claus smiled at him. "Keep talking and you might even earn a cinnamon roll."

Drake grinned and kissed her rosy cheek. "You really do make the best coffee, Bobbi. And Martha makes the absolute best cinnamon rolls on the planet."

Martha, a tall, wiry-headed woman gave him a dubious look as she kneaded a huge lump of bread dough. "I bet you say that to all the girls who ply you with pastries."

A laugh rolled out of him. "Just the pretty ones."

He turned to the third cook and winked. "Like Jo." Joanne, who preferred to be called Jo, sliced a mountain of carrots and celery into sticks and tossed them in a pan filled with ice water. The woman looked like she was capable of handling just about anything the students tossed her way and had in the thirty years she'd worked at the school.

"Okay, take your cinnamon roll and get out of our hair, Drake. We've got better things to do than stand around all day and listen to compliments roll off your silvery tongue," Bobbi said, handing him a plate with a warm cinnamon roll.

Jo fisted her hands on her ample hips and shook a finger at Bobbi. "Speak for yourself! If Drake wants to hang around and wax poetic about how he can't live without us, I'll put him to work peeling spuds. He can at least be useful while he spouts nonsense."

Drake grinned. "I'll take that as my cue to go. Thanks for the coffee and the roll." The three older women told him to have a good day and returned to their work. He hurried down the hall to his classroom and balanced the plate on his mug of coffee as he unlocked the door.

He flicked on the light and inhaled a deep breath, as he did every morning. Some of the classrooms smelled musty and stale, but Drake took pride in making sure his classroom offered a welcoming aroma. Before he left each evening, he sprayed an odor neutralizer. This morning, the air in his classroom held just a hint of citrus from the neutralizer. Underlying tones of crayons, glue, old books, and new notebooks made him smile.

Honestly, he loved his job. Although he was disappointed when his hopes for a pro basketball career came to a screeching halt one blustery February day when he sustained a broken leg and a torn ACL in a massive injury on the court, he couldn't imagine doing anything other than teaching.

Many people wondered why he chose to teach primary grades when he would have made an excellent high school teacher and coach. But Drake's favorite teacher had always been his first grade teacher. When Drake had been recuperating from his injury, Mrs. Edwards had come to visit him. At that time, she'd shared about her plans to retire in a few years and how the school would need a good first-grade teacher, one who could keep up with the students. It was in that moment Drake decided to become an elementary school teacher.

By good fortune or luck, he was never sure which, he landed the job and happily moved back to his hometown of Faraday.

The small town wasn't for everyone, but Drake loved it. He loved the community and the people who lived there. He loved his students and the opportunity to do something that brought him such joy. He loved living close to his family.

Sometimes too close, since he shared an apartment with his brother. The two of them got along well, but the apartment was so tiny, they were constantly bumping into each other. They'd talked about finding a bigger place to rent, but the options in Faraday were limited. Since they both were trying to save their money to invest in a future home of their choosing, they decided to stick with the apartment for a while longer.

And Drake loved Angela Carol, loved her with his whole heart. Afraid she would never see him as anything other than a friend, he tried to set aside his all-consuming feelings for her, but he couldn't. His heart was determined to love Angela Carol. Drake felt helpless to do anything about it, other than silently love her and treasure any little scrap of affection she unwittingly tossed his direction.

He wasn't sure if his plight to spend his life loving a woman who just wanted to be friends was better or worse than his brother's dateless existence. Drew had always been shy and reserved and that hadn't improved with age. His brother had a steady girlfriend in college, but that, too, had ended and Drew hadn't seemed bothered in the least by the split.

The last time Drew had a date was when Drake had talked two women into going out with them when they'd taken a trip to the coast during the summer. Drake had no interest in dating anyone other than Angela, but he'd insisted on taking the two strangers out so Drew could have a good time, except the women were annoying and clingy. Drew declared it was the last date he'd go out on that Drake set up.

Through the years, he'd meddled in his brother's life, teased and tormented him, and forced him into situations that made Drew uncomfortable. Drake had finally concluded it was time to let Drew be Drew. His brother was one of the kindest, biggest-hearted people he'd ever encountered, even if he sometimes came off as gruff or standoffish because of his shyness.

The woman who could draw his sibling out of his shell would win a place of admiration in Drake's heart. He just hoped Drew met someone sooner rather than later. Life was too short to spend it pining away for something... or someone.

Drake sat down at his desk and ate the cinnamon roll then drank his coffee. He took the plate back to the kitchen, refilled the coffee cup and returned to his classroom. After writing the day's lessons on the white board that filled the wall behind his desk, he retrieved the supplies he needed for a science experiment he planned to conduct later that morning and set them on the shelf above the sink at the back of the room. He glanced out the long bank of windows along the side of his room and observed the students playing outside.

With interest, he watched as Angela pulled up and dropped off Nick. She leaned across the seat and said something to Nick before the boy closed the door. By the smiles on both their faces, he assumed she must have said something that humored Nick. That kid had an infectious laugh, one that made everyone around him happy.

Drake wondered, again, about Angela's past. In all the time he'd known her, she'd never once said anything about her husband other than he'd died before Nick was born. He knew she'd grown up in Colorado, an only child, and she frequently mentioned a grandmother in Tennessee. When she spoke of her Granny Carol, though, tears would well in her eyes and she'd quickly change the subject. Someday, he hoped she'd tell him her whole story, if for no other reason than releasing whatever it was that seemed to weigh so heavily on her slim shoulders.

If she'd give him the chance, Drake would gladly bear her burdens, but he couldn't see the capable, independent woman every willingly sharing that much of herself with anyone. Drake doubted Nick even knew the story of Angela's past because he'd heard the boy mention several times that he didn't know anything about his dad except his name was Allen. It was no secret to anyone that Nick desperately wanted a father. But since that required Angela opening her heart and home to someone, Drake feared Nick would never get his wish.

Determined to shake off his melancholy thoughts, Drake pasted on a bright smile as students began trickling into his classroom. Some of the children hung up coats and bags then rushed over to his desk to show him something they'd brought from home or excitedly chatter about what they'd done the previous evening.

Nick was one of the last students to race inside, cheeks rosy from the cold as he and his two friends, Evan and Sean, jostled each other as they hung up their things and made their way to their desks.

As soon as the bell rang, signaling the start of the school day, Drake stood in front of his desk and greeted his class. "Good morning! What kind of day is this going to be?"

"A great day!" the students cheered.

"Awesome!" Drake said, grinning at them. He led the students who wished to participate in the pledge of allegiance. It always filled him with pride to see the students standing so still and respectfully as they gazed up at the flag hanging up in the corner near his desk and recited the familiar words.

When they finished, Drake looked to a little girl with red pigtails. "Megan, it's your turn to lead us in our classroom rules."

Drake had taken the advice of his former teacher when she retired that he establish a set of simple rules for the classroom, stick with them, and remind the students of them often. So each morning, his class recited his five classroom rules. The kids really got into it because there were movements that went along with each rule and he'd turned the rules into a song they could sing.

"Rule one is fun," Megan sang and the rest of the students joined in. They held their hands to their ears and swayed back and forth. "I'll follow directions and listen all day, even when I go out to play."

Drake sang along with the students and made exaggerated movements as they went through the rest of the rules to raise hands before speaking, to walk inside and not run, to be helpful to each other and not hurtful, and to use kind words when speaking to others.

"Great job, everyone. Who finished their homework assignment last night?" he asked and smiled as fourteen students raised their hands in the air. "That's fantastic. Go ahead and take your seats then pass your homework up to the front of the row."

Drake collected the papers and set them in the basket on his desk to grade later. After he wrote down the name of the one absent student, completed the list of the number of lunches needed that day and clipped it in the holder outside his door, he checked his planner to see which student's turn it was for show-and-tell.

He glanced over at a shy little girl who reminded him of Drew at that age. The cascade of her thick brown curls partially hid her face. "Amy, did you bring anything for show-and-tell today?"

The little girl nodded but didn't make eye contact with him.

"Want to share what you brought?" he asked, hunkering down by her desk.

Another slight nod. She chanced a glance up at him and he gave her a reassuring smile and placed a hand on her shoulder.

"Want to go up together?" he asked in a whisper.

She nodded again, this time with a little more enthusiasm. Quickly, she reached into her desk and pulled out something wrapped in a pristine white cloth. Drake took the hand not holding her treasure and led her to the front of the class.

Normally, he sat at his desk and let the student talk about what they brought, but with Amy, he dropped down to his knees beside her. "What do you have to show the class, Amy? I'm excited to see it."

The barest hint of a smile touched her lips as she uncovered her treasure, folding back the cloth. Gingerly, she held it up for everyone to see.

"It's a brown rock," Billy said from his seat nearby.

Drake smiled at Amy and leaned down to whisper in her ear. "It's beautiful, Amy."

While the side of the rock facing the students looked like an ordinary brown blob of stone, the side Amy held toward her contained bright ribbons of color unlike anything Drake had ever seen.

Slowly, Amy turned the big rock over and the students gasped in surprise.

"It looks like a rainbow," Megan said, excitedly clapping her hands as she leaned forward on her desk.

"If I'm not mistaken, that is an iris agate thunderegg, is that right, Amy?" Drake asked the little girl as she slowly walked down the row of desks nearest her so each student could see the wondrous rock up close.

"Yes," Amy said in a quiet voice.

Nick raised his hand and waved it over his head.

"Yes, Nick," Drake asked, glad the boy remembered the rule about raising hands before talking.

"What's a thunderegg, Mr. Miller? Does it come from a bird, like other eggs? I bet it would hurt laying a hard egg like that. My mom takes care of chickens sometimes and I've seen them lay eggs before. It wouldn't be fun to lay a rock."

Drake tried not to laugh. To hide his amusement, he turned to the white board and picked up a red marker. He drew two squiggly lines about a foot apart down the length of the board before he picked up a blue marker and turned back to the students.

"Thundereggs do not come from a bird, Nick, but that was a very good question." Drake pointed to the red lines on his board. When a volcano erupts, lava flows out of it." At the confused look on their faces, he tried to think of something to compare it to. "Have any of you ever seen soda pop flow out of a bottle or glass when it's all foamy?"

Most of the students nodded.

"It's kind of like that. Pressure builds inside and pushes the lava out. Some volcanoes that erupted a long, long time ago had a specific type of lava called rhyolite. It flowed slowly, kind of like if you squeezed a tube of toothpaste just a little too tight to watch it squirt out." Drake pointed to the red lines again then moved his arms downward in slow motion. "So while this lava was slowly flowing down the volcano, gas pockets would form."

"The volcano got the toots!" one little boy said on a giggle and soon the whole class was laughing.

Drake shook his head. "Not that kind of gas, Kale." He opened the cupboard behind his desk and took out a balloon and quickly inflated it. "A gas pocket in the lava would have been kind of like this." He held the balloon up to the board between the two red lines then traced its shape with the blue marker. "As the rock cooled and hardened, the gas would escape, leaving behind an empty shape with cracks." He let the air out of the balloon, drawing more giggles from his students.

After giving them an indulgent smile, he continued with the unplanned science lesson. "Water would bubble up through the rock and carry something called silica. It would turn into a Jello-like substance as it oozed along. Then it would start to fill that empty pocket in layers. The outer layer would be darker, but inside, the Jello-like stuff would blend with minerals and form agates, jaspers, and chalcedony."

"Mr. Miller?" Billy asked, waving his hand over his head. "What's cal… cal's pony?"

"Chalcedony is a form of quartz, usually gray or milky white." Drake took the rock from Amy and held it up so light refracted through the brilliant array of colors. "This is an agate with the colors pressed into bands inside the rock. If we cut a thin slice of this rock and held it up to the light it would shimmer and shine."

"Like glitter?" Emily asked, forgetting to raise

her hand.

"Exactly," Drake said, having too much fun to remind the little girl to raise her hand before speaking.

He handed the rock back to Amy and held the cloth while she placed the rock in the center of it. "Where did you find such a wonderful thunderegg, Amy?"

The little girl gave him a brief glance as she carefully wrapped the rock. "My daddy found it when he was working and brought it home. He let me watch when he broke it open."

"I bet that was lots of fun," Drake said, giving the child a pat on her back as she scurried back to her desk and tucked the rock inside. "What do we say to Amy for bringing in such a fun show-and-tell for us today?"

"Thank you, Amy!" the class chorused.

"Okay, let's get busy with phonics!" Drake said, guiding the class into his lesson plans for the day.

While the students were at recess, he walked around outside, half-frozen, as he watched both his class and the second graders play. At least he didn't have playground duty during the lunch break this week. It wouldn't be his turn for a few more weeks, but by then they'd probably have a foot of snow on the ground and it would be freezing. Then again, it could warm up and be sunny. Although at their elevation, they generally had a white Christmas.

Thoughts of Christmas made Drake wonder what Angela would do for the holiday. The past two years, she'd taken Nick back to visit her grandmother in Tennessee, but her grandmother had passed away in January, so he doubted she'd go south. He thought it odd she never went to Colorado to visit her folks, never talked about them. It also seemed strange Angela had their last name, but perhaps she'd kept it for professional reasons. Since her husband died before Nick was born, it made sense she'd given him her last name. Questions about her past niggled at him again, but he cast them aside as he stood and blew his whistle. Two of the second-graders had engaged in a shoving match.

"That's enough, boys. If you don't want to spend the rest of your recess sitting at a table in the hall, find something better to do than fight."

The two boys stormed off to opposite ends of the playground, but continued glaring at each other. Drake was glad his students all got along. Even if some of his students could be challenging, they all abided by his rules of being kind and respectful to each other. The two troublemakers he'd just whistled at had been in his class the previous year. He hadn't put up with any of their nonsense then, but the new second-grade teacher had yet to figure out how to keep her students in line. He'd tried to help her a few times, but Miss Bradshaw had her own ideas and opinions of how everything should be done.

Drake was glad he hadn't been afraid to take advice from experienced teachers when he first started. Mrs. Edwards had been a jewel, sharing her many years of wisdom with him. If he hadn't taken her tips for success to heart, he wasn't sure he would have survived his first year of teaching.

With a glance at his watch, Drake blew his whistle in three quick blasts, the signal recess was over. The students ran to the door then got into line, with the second-graders leading the way.

When the children settled down and quieted, he opened the door and held it as they filed inside. Drake trailed his students to their room and closed the door behind him. The rest of the day passed quickly. By the time the bell rang at the end of the day, he was as ready to escape as the students.

He walked to the door and smiled at each youngster, wishing them a happy weekend. Before Amy walked out of the room, Drake hunkered down and smiled at her. "Thanks for bringing that cool rock, Amy. It's really awesome."

The little girl beamed with pleasure then hurried out to get on the bus.

Drake released a relieved sigh as the last student left his room. He glanced outside to see if Angela picked up Nick, but it was the vet clinic receptionist. Angela must be in the midst of something, or she never would have sent Tiffany to pick up her son. He started to text her to see if she needed him to help with anything, but stopped himself. She would remind him he already had plans.

Fridays evenings, he and Drew hung out with their good friends, Seth and Rhett. The four of them had kept their weekly get-togethers since Rhett moved back to Faraday a few years ago. Rarely did one of them have a date on Friday night, so they took turns hosting the gathering. They watched movies or ballgames, talked about happenings in the community, and relaxed after a hard week's work.

Drake hurried to finish grading papers, made sure he had his class plans prepared for the coming week, and then cleaned the classroom. He made it a point to spray a disinfectant around the room because Kale had spent most of the day sniffling and wiping his nose on his shirtsleeve instead of the box of tissues he had in his desk.

Thoroughly washing his hands when he finished, he turned off the lights, gathered his things, and hurried out to his SUV.

The overcast sky spit out bits of sleet mingled with little flakes of snow.

"It's only the second week of November," he grumbled turning his face up to the darkening sky. If the temperature continued to plummet and the snow continued to fall, he wondered if the town council would cancel the Veteran's Day parade. It would be a shame if they had to, but no one needed to be out in a blizzard.

In the time it took him to run by the grocery store, then the café where he talked his mom out of a dozen brownies before he drove home, the snow began to fall in earnest. Drake put away the groceries, took his messenger bag to his room, then jumped into a hot shower. He'd been cold since he went out at recess. He dressed in a thermal shirt then added a heavy sweatshirt over the top before sending a text to Rhett that he and Drew still planned to be there for dinner, but they might be late.

He'd just hit send when the door opened and Drew rushed inside along with a blast of cold air.

Drew shook flakes of snow from his hair and brushed it off the shoulders of the navy blue coat of his postal uniform. "I hate snow."

Drake smirked. "Maybe you should have thought about that before you took the job as Faraday's mailman."

Rather than reply, Drew scowled at him and unlaced his work boots then removed his coat. "Give me a minute to take a hot shower and I'll be ready to go. Did you get brownies from Mom?"

"I did. They're packed in a box and ready to go," Drake pointed to a take-out box on the counter in the kitchen. "And before you ask, no, I didn't use all the hot water. Just hustle."

Ten minutes later, they were on their way to Rhett's place on the edge of town. Lolly, the famous camel, stood in the pasture watching them as they drove by.

"Suppose Lolly has welcomed Rhett's new neighbor?" Drake asked as he turned up the lane that led to Rhett's house.

The two brothers glanced at the recently restored Victorian house on the other side of the camel's pasture.

Drew shrugged. "The lights are on, looks like someone is home, so Lolly probably hasn't scared them off yet."

After parking at the back door, Drake grabbed the brownies and the two of them hurried inside along with a flurry of snowflakes.

"What the heck did you two do?" Rhett asked as he glanced outside at the swirling snow. "It's too early for a snowstorm."

Drew glared at their friend. "I certainly didn't order it. You think I enjoy delivering mail in this kind of weather?"

"The temperature dropped ten degrees in the last five minutes," Drake said, removing his coat and giving it a shake outside to dislodge the snow before closing the door. "Is that your famous chili I smell or has Lolly been breathing through the window again?"

The evening went well until Rhett's neighbor called, sounding near hysteria at Lolly being over at her house. Drake thought Rhett ought to call the woman back and apologize, or at least offer to retrieve the camel, but he ignored the call. However, Rhett kept glancing out the window in the direction of the neighbor's house every few minutes. Perhaps Lolly continued going over to the woman's house for a reason, one Rhett needed to discover.

Drake grinned to himself as he dug into the chili and mused over the romantic possibilities that could spring up in Faraday with the arrival of a new woman or two in town. Too bad he couldn't dream of any future possibilities for himself. Hope was a cold, distant stranger when all he really wanted was to be with Angela.

Chapter Four

"Puh-lease, Mommy?" Nick begged, holding his hands beneath his chin and giving Angela his most angelic look. "Pretty please?"

Angela almost laughed at him because no matter how hard he tried to appear innocent, his snapping dark eyes and impish little face always made it look like he was about to embark on a venture of mischief.

"Baby, I don't think it's a good idea," Angela said. She ran her hand through his dark hair then brushed his bangs away from his face.

"But, Mom," he whined, dragging out every letter until it sounded like four words. "It's my turn for show-and-tell. Why can't I take Jasper?"

Angela tucked the snack she'd prepared for him in an insulated bag with her lunch and set it next to her purse by the back door. Nick dogged her steps as she returned to the kitchen and filled an insulated travel mug with sweetened spicy tea. She much preferred it to the taste of coffee and the caffeine in it gave her almost the same jolt as she got from java.

"Honey…" Angela hunkered down so she could look Nick right in the eye. "What happened when you took Shep to school for show-and-tell?"

Nick glanced down and scuffed the toe of his sock back and forth across the kitchen floor. "He got scared and ran over some kids, then made poopies in the hall. Mrs. Beeler was really, really mad."

"That's right. I don't want the same thing to happen with Jasper." Angela had no idea why the bird refused to fly. She'd examined him several times, even X-rayed his wings to make sure he wasn't injured, but the dove seemed perfectly content to stay with her and Nick. She'd planned to take him to the clinic so he wouldn't be alone in the quiet house all day, but a blizzard had kept her from moving him that weekend. Instead, she and Nick had made a place for him in the garage, which was warm and well insulated. He could at least coo at the cats and dog that way.

Oscar and Grover thought he was a new

playmate and Brutus tolerated him as long as he didn't try to land on the dog when he was out of his cage. Nick spent the better part of an hour each evening playing with his animals.

Since the weather had been so cold, Angela relented and let him bring Shep into the garage during playtime, but only if Nick cleaned up any messes that were made. So far, Shep had been good to not leave behind any accidents. Nick faithfully cleaned Jasper's cage after he fed the dog and cats. While he did, Jasper hopped around the garage, playing with an old tennis ball Brutus liked to chew on. Between the bird, the ram, two cats, and the dog, the little boy had plenty of playmates.

However, Angela didn't think it wise to take Jasper to school for a number of reasons, but the most prominent being she didn't want to go inside and face Drake.

He'd practically begged her to spend Thanksgiving with him and his family, saying several friends would join them for dinner at the café. Angela just wasn't in the mood to offer polite conversation. The holidays were a horrible reminder of the darkest point in her past and the faster they came and went, the happier she'd be. She knew she should embrace the season with a heart full of gratitude, but she struggled with it. Struggled to keep up a good front for her son when she really wanted to hibernate from Thanksgiving until after New Year's Day.

On top of that, she couldn't spend time around Drake and not be drawn to him, to his warm and caring spirit, or his fun and exciting personality.

Everything about him intrigued her, fascinated her, and enthralled her.

And that was why she needed to keep her distance.

Despite Drake's convincing arguments and heartfelt pleas she spend Thanksgiving with him, she refused, mumbling some nonsense about already having plans.

Just so she wouldn't be caught in a lie, she quickly booked a hotel room in Portland at a child-friendly hotel near a shopping mall. She and Nick braved the snowy roads down the mountain as soon as he got out of school Wednesday afternoon and spent two nights in Portland. They ate out, went to the movies twice, and Angela took her son to visit Santa at the mall in the midst of all the Black Friday madness. Multiple times she tried to wrangle out of Nick what he asked Santa to bring him for Christmas, but he remained maddeningly tight-lipped on the subject, reminding her that if he told, Santa wouldn't bring it.

Here it was the Monday after Thanksgiving, with a blanket of snow outside and the temperature far below freezing, and Angela was terrified to face her best friend. She'd blown off his efforts at including her in what most likely would have been a wonderful day full of good food and friendship.

Angela had heard through the grapevine at church yesterday that Drew brought Joy Cooke to Thanksgiving dinner. She was glad Drake's brother had taken an interest in the sweet woman. Joy lived up to her name, shining with a special glow from the inside that touched those around her. Drew deserved happiness and Angela sincerely hoped he'd find it with the lovely young woman.

While she was thinking of it, Angela tapped in a note in the planner on her phone to drop by and see Joy. The woman had injured her knee after the first big snowstorm and Drew had found her in the backyard, unable to get inside her house to call for help. Although Angela didn't have time for baking, perhaps she could run by the store and pick up a few things to take Joy. From what she understood, the poor girl had been ordered to stay completely off her feet for a few weeks.

Nick yanked on the hem of her shirt, drawing her attention back to him. "Can't we please take, Jasper, Mom? Everyone will love meeting him."

Angela knew it was too cold to take the bird out, knew she'd have to face Drake. But she also knew taking Jasper to school would make Nick's day.

Hard choice, a sarcastic voice in her head whispered.

"Let me text Mr. Miller first," she said, surrendering to Nick's pleas. "If he says it's okay, then we'll take Jasper."

"Yes!" Nick did a little happy dance while Angela sent Drake a text. He quickly replied that bringing the bird was fine.

She'd half hoped Drake would say it wasn't a good idea and let her off the hook. No such luck. Actually, Drake had asked about the bird a few times and Nick had faithfully provided updates about Jasper to anyone who would listen.

"It looks like Jasper gets to go to school today,"

Angela said, smiling at her son. It was hard to be in a bad mood when his excitement was so infectious. "Hurry and brush your teeth, then pull on your coat and boots while I get Jasper ready to go for a ride." She tucked her phone into one of the pockets of her fleece-lined cargo pants. It annoyed her she couldn't find the pants in women's sizes and had resorted to ordering men's pants online. In the winter, the fleece lining kept her warm when she was out on a call in the cold while the assortment of pockets were perfect for holding supplies she needed at hand. They did nothing to bolster her confidence or make her feel feminine, though. Not that any of that mattered anyway.

With a sigh, she gathered what she'd need for the day and carried it out to her pickup in the garage.

Jasper cooed at her and flapped his wings, as though he knew something was about to happen. "Silly bird," she muttered as she walked past him and returned inside the house.

She tossed one of Nick's fleece blankets in the dryer to warm it then filled a resealable bag with birdseed and dropped it in one of her pockets. While Nick pulled on his coat and boots, she went through the house to make certain everything was turned off that was supposed to be. Assured everything was fine, she joined her son in the laundry room where he zipped up his coat and rammed his hands inside his gloves.

"I'm ready, Mom." Nick picked up his backpack and took it to the pickup, setting it in the back seat. He skipped back to her as she slid her arms into her coat and grabbed the blanket from the dryer.

"Okay, baby. Here's what we're going to do." Angela found it always helped to explain her plans to Nick if she expected his full cooperation. "I want you to climb into your seat and buckle in. I'm going to wrap Jasper in this nice, warm blanket and bring him to you. You'll have to hold him all the way to school. Can you do that?"

"Sure, Mom!" Nick ran to the pickup and climbed into the back seat, buckling himself into his booster seat. "I'm ready!"

"That makes one of us," she grumbled to Jasper as she removed the bird from his cage and gently wrapped the blanket around him. Jasper snuggled down into the warmth and cooed as he looked up at her. She swore if he could have smiled, he would have.

She hastened her steps to the pickup and handed the dove to Nick. "Just keep him warm and calm." Quickly shutting Nick's door, she opened the garage door then started the pickup with her remote so it would be warm when she backed out. She picked up the bird's cage and set it in the back of the pickup then grabbed Jasper's ball, tucking it in one of her pockets before she slid behind the wheel and backed out of the garage.

"How are you two doing back there?" she asked as she pushed the button and watched the garage door close as Brutus and the two cats stared with rapt attention as it rolled down.

"Great, Mom. Jasper closed his eyes, like he's going to take a nap."

"Good," Angela said, distracted. Nerves popped around in her stomach like popcorn kernels in a hot skillet. It was ridiculous to feel that way about seeing Drake. He'd been nothing but kindness itself the past three years. And he was her best friend, the best she'd ever had.

Why, then, did the thought of seeing him today make her want to run back inside her house, lock the door, and never leave again.

"Because you're being an idiot," she whispered as she drove through Faraday.

"What'd you say, Mom?"

"Nothing, honey." Angela pointed to the decorations hanging from the streetlamps. "Aren't the decorations they put up for Christmas pretty?"

"Yep! When are we going to put up our decorations, Mom? Are we going to get a real tree this year? Can we make a paper chain to put on it? Evan's mom helped him make a paper chain to count down to Christmas. Can we do that? Do we have paper, Mom? I bet we could get some at the store tonight. Can we, Mom? Huh?"

Angela swallowed back a sigh. "We won't be able to do any of that tonight, baby, but we'll definitely put up a tree before Christmas and some decorations. We've got almost four weeks before Christmas arrives, so there's no need to rush."

Nick remained quiet the rest of the way to school. Angela hated to disappoint him, but she couldn't think about decorating the house right now. It was bad enough she'd promised Tiffany she could decorate the clinic today. Angela would have to climb up in the storage shed where they'd stored all the decorations and find the box for the clinic. Maybe she could send Brad, her vet tech, to do it.

"Okay, baby. I'm going to get out and carry in Jasper's cage. I want you to wait right here with him until I come back. We can't let him get cold, so be sure you stay in the pickup where it's warm."

Nick rolled his eyes. "Duh, Mom. I know."

"Hey, buster, you need to dial down the sass, or I'll take Jasper back home right now."

"Sorry, Mom." Nick appeared repentant as he held the bird.

Angela got out, but saw Nick whispering to Jasper. She had no doubt he complained about his mean, grouchy mom. She retrieved the cage and carried it inside the school, heading straight to Drake's classroom. The door was open so she didn't bother knocking.

Instead, she stepped inside and watched as he wrote the day's assignments on the white board. That man could make an oxford shirt and a pair of dark slacks sure look good.

Suddenly, he turned around and caught her ogling him.

Heat seared her cheeks, but she ducked her head and held up the cage. "Where would you like to put Jasper?"

"How about on this table?" Drake moved a caddy full of craft supplies from a large table near the window.

"Perfect. Do you have some newspapers?" she asked, carrying the cage across the room.

"No, but I've got a bin full of papers that need to be recycled. Jasper can have them."

"That'll work." Angela had Drake set papers down on the table before she added the cage. The cage didn't take up a lot of space width wise, but it was as tall as many of Drake's students with three different perches, giving Jasper plenty of room to fly and move. Angela lined the bottom of the cage with the papers Drake handed to her then filled Jasper's little food dish with birdseed she took from the bag in her pocket. While Drake took care of getting water for the bird, she dug in another pocket for his ball and set it in the cage.

"Nick's waiting in the pickup for me with the dove." Angela cleared her throat, finding it hard to speak when Drake stood with his arms across his chest, giving her a look she couldn't interpret. All she knew was the light glowing in his gorgeous blue eyes and the smile accenting the dimple in his chin made her want to obliterate the distance between them, both literally and figuratively. She longed to give in to her heart's demands and kiss him.

But her heart had been wrong before and had lost its voting rights, as far as Angela was concerned. She spun around and hurried outside to where she'd parked in front of the door. If she didn't hurry and move, she'd be blocking the school buses when they started to arrive.

She opened Nick's door and took the bird from him. Her son jumped down, grabbed his backpack and held out his hands for Jasper. For a moment she hesitated to give him the bird, but decided to trust him. He'd get the dove safely to the classroom. "Go straight to Mr. Miller's room, okay? No dilly-dallying."

Nick didn't say anything, but she caught the roll of his eyes as he turned around and carried Jasper inside the school.

Angela hurried to park her pickup in the parking lot then jogged back inside. She returned to Drake's classroom to find him kneeling on the floor near the table with the cage, holding Jasper while the bird cooed.

"Look, Mom! Jasper remembers Mr. Miller from the day we rescued him. Isn't it cool?"

Angela seriously doubted the bird remembered Drake, but she wouldn't correct her son. Not when the bird looked perfectly content in the man's strong hands.

"It'll take a minute for the cage to warm up," Angela said, removing her coat and draping it over one of two chairs in the back of the room where parents visiting the classroom sat. "We shouldn't have brought him out on such a cold day, but Nick really wanted to share him for show-and-tell today."

"I think Jasper will settle in just fine." Drake continued to stroke a light hand over the bird's back. "If you like, you can leave him here all day. It won't bother me to have him and it might be fun for the students."

"Oh, I don't know. It might upset Jasper with all the noise and activity."

Nick ran over to her and wrapped his arms around her waist, tipping his head back to stare into her face with the most adorable smile. "Please, Mom? Can we keep Jasper all day?"

Inclined to say no, she gave Drake a questioning glance. When he nodded his head, as though urging her to agree, she felt outnumbered by the man and boy she loved. "Let's see how Jasper does during show-and- tell. If he seems fine, he can stay. If he's upset, I'll take him when I leave."

"Deal," Nick said, giving her a tight squeeze before going back to stand next to Drake. "Jasper is going to love it here."

"You can go outside and play until school starts, if you want, Nick," Drake said, smiling at the boy. "I'll take good care of your bird."

Nick tugged his stocking cap from his pocket and yanked it over his head as he ran toward the door.

"Walk indoors, Nick. Walk!" Drake called after him with a chuckle.

Angela felt like her feet had taken root to the floor when Drake stood and made his way to her, still holding the dove. He didn't say anything, just melded that mesmerizing gaze of his to hers until he stood directly in front of her.

Unsettled, she wanted to back away, but couldn't force herself to move.

"Did you have a good Thanksgiving?" Drake asked in a conversational tone.

"It was nice," Angela said, realizing she spoke the truth. She couldn't even remember the last time she'd been to Portland. Doc Johnson had promised to be on call in case anyone needed a vet over the weekend, which no one did. Desperately, Angela had needed time away from Faraday, time to hang out with Nick and enjoy her little boy.

"Nick told me about all the things you saw and did. It sounds like he had a great time going to the movies, eating out, and visiting Santa at the mall."

Angela nodded. "By chance, he didn't tell you what he wants Santa to bring him, did he?"

"Nope. And I feel it's only fair to warn you, some of the kids have been debating whether Santa is real. Nick has been a staunch supporter of Santa, but I thought you ought to know in case he brings it up."

No longer believing in Santa? Angela sank down on a little plastic chair and drew in a long breath. She'd been seven when she decided Santa no longer existed. Nick was only... six. Tears stung her eyes as she thought about how quickly her little boy was growing up. First he'd stop believing in Santa and the Easter Bunny, then she'd blink and he'd be asking for the car keys to take a girl out to the prom.

"No, no, no," she said, burying her face in her hands, distraught as she envisioned how rapidly the future would fly by and it would be no time at all before Nick would leave for college.

"Hey, Angel, are you okay?" Drake asked, hunkering down next to her and rubbing comforting circles across her back.

The touch from Drake that was meant to be comforting sent every nerve ending in her body into a frenzied dance. There was only so much she could take before something had to give.

"I'm great," she croaked in a voice that sounded strained, even to her ears.

"If you say so," Drake said, then stood and moved back a few steps.

She sucked in a cleansing breath then looked

up at him. Darn it! Why did the man have to get more handsome every time she saw him? How unfair was that?

She was sure she looked like a disaster and she hadn't even dealt with a patient yet today. Her hair was twisted into a messy bun at the back of her head, she didn't have on any makeup unless a quick swipe of mascara counted, and she'd grabbed the first clean scrub top her hand found that morning, yanking it on over a purple long-sleeved thermal shirt. The scrub top just happened to be one with a flurry of cute little forest animals on it, with everything from foxes and owls to bunnies and lavender-backed hedgehogs.

Even if she'd wanted to catch Drake's eye, which she most certainly did not, a harried mom wearing outrageous scrub tops with men's winter cargo pants didn't exactly scream dating material for a good-looking single guy.

"How about you? Did you have a good Thanksgiving?" she asked, wishing the bell would ring and the students would pour inside so she'd have an excuse to remain silent.

"It was okay," Drake said. He stared at her as though he searched for something in her expression, as though he could see into her mind and heart.

Troubled by the intensity of his gaze, she turned and looked out the window at the children on the playground. "Only okay? Didn't you have a good day with your family and friends?"

Drake moved beside her. Good grief, he even smelled delicious. There, among the fresh scent he managed to maintain in his classroom and the wafts of glue, crayons, and paper, she caught a whiff of something masculine and entirely enthralling. What was he trying to do to her?

She shoved her hands into the front pockets of her scrubs before she did something crazy like wrap them around the back of Drake's neck and pull his head down for a sizzling kiss.

When he cleared his throat and shifted away from her, she wondered if he'd somehow read her mind. "Everyone was there, except my best friend and my best little buddy." He gave her a pointed glance. "I really did miss you being there, Angela."

"I'm sorry, Drake. I just needed to get away for a day or two and spend some time with Nick."

He nodded. "I know and I can't fault you for it. In fact, you really are a great mom to Nick and he's an awesome kid because of it."

Surprised by his compliment when she so often felt like a huge parental failure, Angela placed a hand on his arm and gave it a gentle squeeze. "Thank you for saying that."

"I wouldn't say it if it wasn't true." Drake cleared his throat again and looked down at the bird he continued to hold. "Drew brought Joy Cooke to dinner. That was something of a shock."

"Do they make a cute couple?" she asked, turning back to the window then glancing at Drake when he chuckled.

"Cute? Drew would have an acute attack of something if someone referred to him as part of a cute couple. But yeah, they do make a cute couple. It's obvious they care about each other. Drew acts as though he's finally found a missing piece of himself and Joy seems equally as loopy over my brother." Drake offered her a rascally grin. "There's just no accounting for some people's taste."

"Oh, give Drew a break," Angela said, knowing Drake was only teasing. The affection and devotion the Miller brothers shared ran deep, and was evident to anyone who knew them. "He deserves to grab onto whatever happiness comes his way and I like Joy. She's one of the nicest, happiest humans I've ever met."

"She really is. I helped Drew over at her house a few times since she got hurt. She really is an upbeat, sweet gal. And she's got that weird donkey and equally strange pup."

"Oh, I like Pete, and little Bacon is fun." Angela nudged Drake with her elbow. "You just want a donkey of your own."

"Nope, not at all. But I might settle for a dove." Drake smiled when Jasper cooed, as though he agreed with the idea. "Honestly, Angela, I don't mind if you leave him here all day."

"We'll see how he does with the kids." The ringing of the bell kept her from having to say more.

She moved to the back corner and stood by the chair where she'd left her coat. With a smile, she greeted the students and even bent down to talk to a few who came over to ask her questions about her clinic and the animals she treated.

Drake handed Jasper to Nick then took his place in front of the classroom. After they went through their usual morning routine, he grinned at Nick and motioned him to come to the front of the class.

"It's Nick's turn for show-and-tell and he brought a special friend along today." Drake winked at Angela then moved to the side of the room and leaned against a bookcase while Nick talked all about finding Jasper outside and taking care of him at home.

"What does he like to eat?" Kale asked.

Nick stroked Jasper as he looked at his classmates. "Bird seed, mostly, but he gets treats like pieces of apple or hard-boiled eggs and broccoli."

A few of the kids wrinkled their noses at the thought of eating broccoli.

"Can he do any tricks?" Megan asked, leaning forward on her desk, trying to stretch far enough to pet Jasper.

Nick moved closer to her and showed her how to gently pet the bird. "He plays with my cats and dog, and Shep. And he can chase a ball."

"I want to see!" Billy said.

Nick looked toward his mother. She walked to the front of the room and took Jasper from him. With slow steps she walked past each student's desk and those who wanted could pet the dove before she returned to the front. She set Jasper down on the table and Nick took his ball from the cage and rolled it toward the bird.

Jasper bobbed his head and wiggled his back end as he scurried toward the ball then bonked it with his beak, sending it back toward Nick.

Several students clapped and cheered. "Do more, please?" Emily asked.

Angela glanced at Drake and he nodded, giving permission for the disruption to his class and schedule.

"If you all quietly come up here, you can gather around the table and watch him play," Angela said.

The students made slightly less noise than a herd of stampeding elephants as they rushed to encircle the table where Jasper and Nick played ball. After a few minutes of watching, more students asked questions and Angela let Nick provide the answers. Finally, she glanced at the clock and picked up Jasper. The bird cooed and ducked his head beneath his wing then stared up at her.

She tucked him inside his cage, along with his ball, and closed the door. She handed Drake the leftover birdseed, whispered he could call if he had any problems during the day with the bird, and smiled at the class. "Jasper is going to hang out with you all today, but remember, he doesn't like loud noises."

"We'll be quiet, Mrs. Carol, we promise!" Billy assured her.

Nick gave her a hug then returned to his seat with the rest of the students.

"Have a great day," Angela said to the class, although her gaze landed on Drake as she grabbed her coat and headed out the door.

The day passed in a flurry of appointments that left her exhausted. She made it to school as the last bus pulled away from the sidewalk. Nick waved at her from where he played on the swings and jumped off, running over to her when she crossed the parking lot.

"Hey, baby. Did you have a good day?" she asked, wrapping an arm around him and pulling Nick against her side.

"I had a great day, Mom. Everyone loves Jasper and I got all my math right and Mr. Miller shoved pencils through a bag of water and it didn't even leak a single drop."

"Wow! That sounds like an exciting day." Angela took his hand and headed toward the front door of the school.

"Aren't we going home, Mom?" Nick asked, skipping along beside her.

"We need to get Jasper." Angela opened the door and held it while Nick scurried inside. If only she had a tenth of his energy, she wouldn't be wishing she could curl up on her bed and take a quick nap. The last time she'd had a nap was just before Nick was born, and that was only because Granny forced her to rest.

"I thought Jasper was staying here," Nick said, as he hopped his way down the hall toward the first grade classroom.

Angela gave him a studying glance. "Why would you think that, honey?"

"Well, Mr. Miller said Jasper can stay as long as you want to leave him here." Nick took her hand and yanked on it. "Please, Mom, can Jasper stay? He liked the kids and cooed all day. It was awesome!"

"All day?" Angela asked, wondering how disruptive the bird had been to Drake's class. Why hadn't he called and asked her to come get the bird.

Stubborn man probably didn't want to disturb her.

She rushed into the classroom to find Drake bent over talking to Jasper as the bird chased his ball across the top of the table.

"Hey, Angela! Jasper is awesome. Can I keep him?" Drake asked, shooting her a boyish grin that weakened her knees to the point she thought she might collapse.

She reached out and grasped the edge of the nearest shelf for support. "Keep him? Nick said he cooed all day. Didn't that drive you nuts? Distract the kids?"

Drake stood and smiled. "Just the opposite. The more Jasper cooed, the quieter the students were while they worked. I've never had them so settled and well behaved before. It's like Jasper is a magical kid whisperer."

Angela laughed. "Are you sure, Drake? I mean, you'll have to clean his cage and feed him, and exercise him and…"

He waved a dismissive hand her way. "I let the kids take him out of the cage and play with him twice today. Jasper loved it and so did they. Nick supervised, of course."

Nick pulled on Angela's hand, dragging her away from the only thing helping her remain upright. "Yeah, Mom, it was so cool. Jasper's like our class mascot. You know, we've got the falcon for the school, but Jasper can be just ours, for the class." Her son gave her one of his pleading looks that would have softened the stoniest heart. Even the Grinch couldn't have resisted his smile. "Please, Mom. Let Jasper stay. Please?"

Drake tossed her a look only slightly less pleading but one she found entirely alluring. "Yeah, please. Let Jasper stay. Pretty please?"

Angela shook her head then sighed in resignation. "How can I say no to that?"

Drake gave Nick a high five then Nick hugged Angela around her waist.

Angela gave them both pointed looks. "However, if Jasper becomes disruptive or he isn't happy here in class, he comes back home. Understood?"

"Yes, ma'am," Drake said.

"Yes, ma'am," Nick mimicked, then hugged Angela again. "Thanks, Mom!"

"You're welcome, baby. Come on. I don't have any more patients today, so I thought we could string some lights around outside the house, if you want."

Nick whooped with joy, then clapped a hand over his mouth and shot Drake an apologetic look.

Drake reached out and ruffled his hair. "It's okay, Nick. Christmas lights are worth getting excited about." He turned to Angela. "Anything special I need to know about Jasper's care?"

"No. I'll bring his bag of feed when I drop Nick off tomorrow. You should have plenty for him for tonight. His cage needs to be cleaned at least once a day and that has been Nick's job and can continue to be if you want," Angela said, giving her son a motherly look. "He needs to stay warm and he'll want a dark space at night. You can drape that blanket we brought in this morning over the cage at night to block the light and make it warmer for him.

He should be just fine right there unless you want to move the cage somewhere else."

"I think on the table will work great for now. The kids still have room do to their crafts around the cage and Jasper can strut his stuff when they aren't using the table." Drake walked her to the door with a strange look on his face. He seemed hesitant to see them go, but Angela had no reason to linger. When he continued studying her, she glanced away.

Drake cleared his throat. "I'll take good care of him."

"I know you will. Otherwise, I wouldn't leave him." Angela smiled at him then took Nick's hand in hers. She needed to escape Drake's presence before she did something ridiculous, like rest her head against his strong chest or beg him to hold her for a while. "Come on, Nick. There's a ladder at home with my name on it."

Chapter Five

Angela carried the last box of decorations down from the loft in the storage building and set it on her small front porch. Granny would have referred to it as a veranda, since it only stretched about five feet on either side of her front door, but around Faraday, it was the front porch. Nick alternated between excitedly carrying boxes and tubs with decorations inside and racing around the yard, asking her if she was ready to hang the lights yet.

Truthfully, Angela hated climbing on ladders.

She would have gladly paid someone to do the job while she was at work, but Nick was so excited about helping, she couldn't deny him the opportunity.

With effort, she packed the ladder to the front corner of the house. She decided to start there and do the steep pitch of the roof on the side of the house while there was still a bit of light outside before she did the easy stringing of lights across the front. Doc Johnson had installed a series of hooks under the eaves that made hanging a simple thing, at least in theory. Any time she had to climb up on a ladder higher than her head it made her dizzy and complicated the task.

With a string of white lights in her hand, she'd just placed her foot on the ladder when a vehicle pulled up and parked in front of the house.

Nick waved with enthusiasm and rushed over to greet Drake as he stepped out and headed their way. He'd exchanged his dress slacks and button down shirt for a pair of jeans and a heavy sweatshirt beneath a thick wool coat. He tugged on a stocking cap and took gloves from his pockets as he walked toward her.

Angela stepped back and fisted one hand on her hip. "What are you doing here? Is it Jasper? Is he okay?"

"He's great. Don't worry." Drake settled his hands on her shoulders. The touch, even through layers of gloves and coats, made a shiver race down her spine.

"Then what's up?" she asked, irritated by her reaction to him, by how glad she was to see him.

"I thought you might like some help with the lights," Drake gave her a crooked grin. "I'm practically an expert at it, you know."

She offered him a dubious look. "I did not know you were an expert. I suppose that can only be proven through observation." In spite of her need to be a strong, independent woman, she gladly handed him the strand of lights and watched him scale the ladder. It took him no time at all to hang the lights along the high pitch line then move on to the front of the house. He was tall enough he could easily reach the hooks beneath the eaves without standing on the stepstool she'd carried outside. Angela and Nick handed him the lights then together they strung strands around the porch posts and across the balustrade.

"Shall we plug them in and see how it looks?" Drake asked, reaching for the power strip he'd set at the corner of the porch near an outlet.

"Plug them in, Mr. Miller," Nick said, unable to stand still as he bounced around in the snow.

"I think you should do it, Nick," Drake said, glancing at Angela for confirmation.

She nodded, unable to speak as she watched Drake hold out an arm and her son rush over to him. Drake set a hand on Nick's back and helped him plug in the heavy cord.

"Okay, Nick. On the count of three, flip that red switch on the power strip. Ready?" Drake asked. At the boy's eager nod, Drake stood and walked over to Angela.

It seemed the most natural thing in the world when he took her hand in his and together they started counting. "One, two… three!" Angela cheered when the lights came on, illuminating her house and casting a warm glow through the evening shadows.

"Thank you, Drake! So much!" Impulsively, she gave him a hug then pulled back when Nick ran over and threw his arms around both of them, holding them close together.

"Mom, can Mr. Miller stay for dinner?"

"Oh, baby, I'm sure he has other plans." Angela glanced at Drake, wanting him to stay but also afraid he would.

"But, Mom, we're having chicken and dumplings and I bet Mr. Miller likes them, too. Please?"

Angela ignored her sons pleading and forced herself to meet Drake's gaze. "We'd love to have you stay if you don't have other plans. It's nothing fancy, but we have plenty."

"I'd like to stay, thank you," Drake said, giving her a look full of something she hesitated to acknowledge or decipher.

"Let's get the chores out of the way before we eat, Nick. Then we can stay inside this evening and maybe set up a few of the decorations." Angela glanced at Drake. "You don't have to help. Feel free to go inside and warm up."

"I'll tag along with you," he said, following her as she went to the barn to feed Shep while Nick fed and watered the cats and Brutus. After she dumped out Shep's water pan and refilled it, the two of them made their way inside the garage where Nick raced back and forth past her pickup with the cats and dog chasing him.

Brutus, who generally barked at strangers and growled at men, ran right over to Drake and sat down, wagging his tail like a feather duster across the concrete floor.

"Hey, Brutus. How's it hangin', my man?" Drake got down on the floor to pet the dog and both cats before he stood and brushed animal hair from his clothes. He followed Nick and Angela inside.

Her son adored Drake, her animals trusted him, and yet she refused to get close to him. Nothing good could come of it. Nothing at all.

Except maybe you'd finally experience true love, a traitorous voice whispered in her head.

"Hush," she snapped, then realized she'd spoken aloud.

Nick and Drake both stared at her as they removed their coats and hung them up.

Cheeks blazing with embarrassment, she spun around and busied herself washing her hands at the sink. "Sorry, my tummy is telling me it's ready for dinner." It wasn't an outright lie. She was hungry and her stomach was grumbling at her, but that had more to do with nerves and far less to do with the delicious smells emanating from the kitchen.

"Come see my room, Mr. Miller. Mom helped me paint the ceiling since the last time you came to visit." Nick tugged on Drake's hand and the two of them disappeared down the hall.

Angela could hear the rumble of Drake's voice, although she couldn't make out the words. For once, she was glad for Nick's "come see" age because it gave her a few moments to gather her unraveling composure before Drake returned to the kitchen.

He'd stopped in the bathroom and washed his hands, pushing up the sleeves of his sweatshirt to reveal corded forearms. She wondered what in the world he did in his spare time to stay so strong and in shape. If she didn't spend her days on the go, wrestling with unhappy animals of all sizes, she'd definitely be forced to invest in a gym membership. Come to think of it, Faraday didn't have a gym.

"Anything I can do to help?" Drake asked from beside her, startling her from her musings.

Heart pounding both from her shock and his proximity, she tipped her head toward a cupboard by the sink. "Nick's job is to set the table, but you can pour drinks. He and I usually drink milk. I have soda, juice, or water if you'd rather have something else." Angela spoke so quickly her words nearly blended together.

Drake grinned. "Milk it is. It does a body good, right?" He patted his trim abs, then turned to get glasses out of the cupboard.

Angela squeezed her eyes shut, attempting to subdue her wayward thoughts. Drake just had to draw her attention to his form. One she'd envisioned multiple times when she tossed and turned at night, unable to sleep.

Thankfully, Nick ran into the room, hands partially dry from his haphazard use of the towel in the bathroom, drawing her attention away from her nearly overwhelming attraction to Drake.

Nick hurried to set the table as he chattered away, diffusing some of the tension that threatened to suffocate Angela as she prepared a green salad and scooped chicken and dumplings into a serving dish.

"This looks great, Angela," Drake said as he held out her chair and waited for her to take a seat.

She gaped at the chair, as though it was a foreign object she'd never before seen in her house, then silently slid onto the seat. No one had ever held out a chair for her, made her feel special, like Drake did with just a few sweet looks or kind gestures.

"Mom cooks good," Nick said, reaching out to take Angela's hand then clasping Drake's. The little boy looked expectantly at her, waiting for her to say grace.

Angela managed to offer a brief prayer without tripping over the words. The feel of Drake's hand holding hers made her pulse gallop so furiously, she was sure Shep could probably hear it thumping like a bass drum clear out in the barn.

"How did you have time to make such an incredible meal?" Drake asked after he took a bite of the chicken and dumplings on his plate.

"I'm a slow cooker queen," Angela said, pointing to one small and two large slow cookers lined up on her counter. "I toss ingredients in before we leave in the morning, set it to low, and come home to a hot meal. It's the only way this poor boy gets anything beyond peanut butter sandwiches or cereal for dinner."

"I like peanut butter sandwiches, but only with grape jelly or berry jam," Nick said. "My mom made jam this summer. We bought berries from Mrs. Pith. She smells like medicine and her hair looks like one of those scrubber things Mom uses on her big skillet." The boy gestured toward his head. "But she grows good berries and she gave me a thingamajig when we went to her store to get the berries."

"A thingamajig?" Drake asked, looking from Nick to Angela.

"Can I show him, Mom?" Nick asked, already halfway out of his chair.

"Go ahead." Angela nodded.

Nick raced out of the room and quickly returned with a toy someone had obviously made. A big nail that had been welded to a thin metal plate formed the bottom and stand. On top of that a stick figure man made of bended wire held a piece of curved metal with a small metal ball at each end. The man bobbed back and forth in a never-ending effort to keep his balance.

"Aw, that kind of thingamajig. Drew and I used to have one of those we played with sometimes." Drake grinned at Nick as the boy set the toy on the counter and returned to his dinner.

After they finished eating, Angela expected Drake to leave. Instead, he gave her a hand with the dishes while Nick did his homework. Then he offered to help her unpack the boxes of Christmas decorations.

"No, you've done enough already, Drake. I'm sure you have better things to do than stay here and dig through these dusty boxes with us." Angela wasn't sure she could handle spending too much time around Drake and maintain what little bit of sanity she still possessed. He was too handsome, too sweet, too wonderful. Oh, she knew Drake had his flaws, just like anyone, but from her viewpoint, he was an amazing guy.

"I have nothing pressing I need to do this evening and it would be my privilege to help you, if you want me to stay," Drake said, following Angela into the living room. Half a dozen boxes and plastic storage tubs waited to be opened and the contents explored.

Angela really didn't want to decorate the house, and the last thing she needed was to spend an additional hour or two with Drake, but she couldn't say no. Not when Nick practically danced off one foot to the other with anticipation and Drake appeared nearly as excited.

"Go for it," Angela said, sliding a box toward Drake.

"Yay!" Nick cheered as he opened a box and began removing garlands.

While Nick and Drake draped garlands around doorways and over the fireplace mantel, she unpacked the breakable decorations like an old mason jar that had a winter scene nestled inside it, complete with iridescent glitter for snow.

Angela opened a small box and took a deep breath as a wave of nostalgia washed over her. Suddenly, she was a little girl again, sitting in her Granny's kitchen, cutting out gingerbread cookies and listening to Andy Williams croon Christmas carols as a record played in the background.

"What's that scent?" Drake asked, as he knelt on the floor beside where she sat on the couch with the box still on her lap.

"Bayberry. My grandma always made her own candles each year and burned them throughout the season. She…" Angela took a shaky breath, determined to get her spiraling emotions in check.

The holiday scent filled the space around her, making it impossible to think of anything other than her grandmother and how much she missed her. This would be her first Christmas without Granny. The woman had been Angela's rock her entire life. Now that rock was gone, leaving a big, empty hole in her place.

Unable to stop the tears welling in her eyes, Angela jumped when Drake brushed the salty drops from her cheeks with his thumbs.

"Hey, it's okay, Angel," he whispered, glancing over to where Nick danced to a silly Christmas song playing on Angela's phone and waved a garland around his head. "If you need to cry, cry. I know you miss your granny. It must be hard trying to get through this holiday season without her."

Angela couldn't even speak around the lump lodged in her throat. She set the box on her lap aside, jumped to her feet, and ran to her bedroom. She rushed into the bathroom, shut the door, and sat down on the edge of the tub where she gave herself a few minutes to release the grief she'd held in since she returned from Granny's funeral in January.

When the sobs subsided, she took several cleansing breaths then stood and rinsed her flushed face with cool water. A glance in the mirror assured her she looked even worse than she imagined. She toweled her face dry, reapplied mascara, and even took a minute to take her hair out of the bun at the back of her head and brush through it. She left it down and pinched her cheeks to give them a bit of color. At least she'd taken time to change out of her work clothes when she and Nick arrived home earlier.

She didn't know why she cared how she looked. Drake probably thought she was a basket case anyway. With one more deep breath, she returned to the living room to find Drake and Nick making a paper chain with wrapping paper she'd stored in a plastic tub.

"Look, Mom! We're making a countdown chain. Mr. Miller says I get to take one off every day starting tomorrow until Christmas. Isn't that cool?" Nick asked as he sat on his knees and reached for another strip of paper that Drake had cut.

"That's great, baby." Angela sank onto the floor next to Nick and placed a hand on his back.

Drake gave her a questioning look, but she couldn't meet his gaze. Not right now when her heart felt so raw and vulnerable.

When Nick and Drake finished with the paper chain, Drake helped her son drape it across the windowsill by the kitchen table. Together, they washed the glue from their hands while Angela picked up the scissors and leftover strips of paper.

Angela got out bowls and spooned chocolate lava cake from the slow cooker into them. She served the dessert topped with a scoop of vanilla ice cream.

She set a bowl on the table for Nick and poured

half a glass full of milk for him. "I know you like chocolate," she said as she handed Drake a bowl of cake and a spoon.

He took a bite and looked like he might kiss her. Instead he hurriedly took another bite. "I think that might be the best chocolate cake I've ever had, but don't you dare tell my mother I said that."

Angela laughed as she made two cups of tea, then took a seat at the table. The cake was rich and delicious, just what she needed, just how she imagined Drake's kisses might taste.

Aggravated with herself and her wayward thoughts about her best friend, she asked Drake how Seth's grandpa was doing since he'd returned to the ranch after having hip surgery.

"Apparently, Sam ran off one nurse in tears and Seth isn't fond of her replacement." Drake shrugged as he spooned another bite of cake. "We'll see how long it lasts."

Nick finished his last bite of cake so Angela sent him to get ready for bed. While her rambunctious little boy took a bath, Angela tried to find the words to apologize to Drake for falling apart earlier. Nothing came to mind, so she quietly ate her cake. Drake finished his and drained his cup of tea then carried his dishes to the sink.

Angela scrambled to come up with something to say. "I'm sorry, Drake, about earlier. I didn't mean to…"

Before she finished her apology, Drake pulled her up into his arms and kissed her forehead. "I'm sorry you're having a hard time, Angel. If you ever need someone just to listen, I'm always here. You know that, right?"

She nodded as tears once again pricked her eyes and robbed her of the ability to speak.

Drake kissed her forehead again then gave her a tight hug. "I'm gonna go, but if you want more help with the decorations or anything at all, just say the word."

"No, Drake, you've done too much as it is," she whispered, trying her best to hold back her tears. It felt so good, so right, to be in Drake's arms. To accept the comfort he offered and draw from the deep well of his strength.

Because she never wanted it to end, she hastily pulled away from him. "Thank you for everything, Drake. I really am sorry I…" Her voice broke and she turned away before she started crying again.

"It's okay, Angel."

She felt his warmth envelop her as he stepped close behind her and bent his head so his breath caressed her ear. "Anytime you need me, anytime at all, I'll always be here."

Eyes closed, she nodded her head. Cold seeped around her when he moved away. She heard him holler at Nick to have a good night before the front door opened then clicked shut.

Angela dropped down on the nearest chair and leaned back, distraught. For the sake of her son she had to pull herself together and get her head on straight. Not just because of her grief over losing Granny and the pain of her past, but because Drake Miller had no place in her future. None at all.

Chapter Six

Drake set a basket of folded laundry on his bed then changed out of the slacks and sweater he'd worn to church. He yanked on his cold-weather running gear and dug in the closet for his running shoes.

Every Sunday, he and Drew had lunch with their parents at their home following church services and often spent the afternoon watching football with their dad while doing laundry. Their apartment didn't have a hook-up for a washer or dryer, and neither of them liked going to the laundromat in town. In trade for letting them do their laundry there, the two brothers often tackled projects their mom wanted done that their dad purposely avoided getting around to completing.

Today had been no different. After eating his mom's pot roast with carrots, potatoes, and more than his share of hot rolls, buttered corn, and apple cake, he and Drew had hung the outside lights and carried the Christmas tree decorations along with the artificial tree down from the attic.

Since his parents both worked so many hours at the café, they kept their Christmas decorations minimalistic at home, although they went all out at the restaurant.

While their dad hollered at the losing team during the football game, Drake and Drew helped their mom decorate the tree in between loads of laundry.

By mid-afternoon, Drake felt tied in knots. Drew had taken great pleasure in tattling about how Drake had messed things up the previous weekend between Rhett and his beautiful neighbor, Cedar. Rhett had been trying, for reasons no one knew, to keep the fact he was Cedar's camel-owning neighbor a secret from the woman. Drake and Drew had joined Rhett and Seth at Cedar's house to hang her lights then stayed for dinner. Without thinking, Drake accidentally blurted out that Rhett owned Lolly. The moment he'd opened his big mouth, he wished he could snatch back the words, but it was too late. Cedar wasn't speaking to Rhett and Rhett was barely speaking to Drake.

On top of that fiasco, Drew was acting strange about Joy and Drake couldn't get Angela out of his thoughts for more than five minutes at a time.

The other night when she'd rushed off to cry alone in her room, he'd wanted to go to her, to comfort her. Not because he wanted to deal with a woman's tears, but because he'd known she needed someone, needed the comfort of another human assuring her everything would be okay. He knew she missed her grandmother, but he had a feeling what bothered her included far more than her grief over her beloved granny. Every effort he made to get her to talk to him resulted in her drawing away. Since she stopped every day after school to check on Jasper, he both dreaded and looked forward to the moment she'd walk through his classroom door.

Frustrated she wouldn't open up to him, give him a chance to be a true friend to her, he just wanted to punch or kick something. Since that was out of the question, he'd decided to go for a run and hopefully work off some of the tension coiling inside him.

Normally, Drake loved the holiday season, relished every part of it. From the excitement of his students to the traditional community activities, he enjoyed every special moment. He typically got along great with Drew and his friends. Yet, here he was barely speaking to his brother or Rhett and dreading the coming weeks of the Christmas season all because of his feelings for a woman who saw him as a friend. Not even a good friend, just someone she talked to about everything except the things that really mattered.

Drake tucked his cell phone into a pocket in his shirt's sleeve and zipped it shut then grabbed a set of Bluetooth-enabled ear warmers.

"I'm going for a run," he said to Drew as he poked his head inside his brother's bedroom.

Drew angrily slammed a drawer as he put away clean clothes. He glanced over his shoulder and scowled at Drake. "Are you nuts? It's freezing outside and it's supposed to start snowing again."

"I know, but I just need…" Drake didn't know what to say, didn't know what he needed beyond Angela. "I'll be fine. Want me to bring back anything for dinner?"

"If it's fine with you, I'll make grilled cheese sandwiches and soup. It's my turn to cook isn't it?"

"Yeah, and that's fine. Thanks, Drew." Drake turned and left the apartment. Outside, the frigid temperatures made him shiver. He'd probably give himself pneumonia, but at that moment he didn't really care.

He tugged the ear warmers on, chose an eighties rock station, and stretched his muscles. When he started jogging down the sidewalk a few minutes later, an unbidden picture of Angela walking into the living room the other night with her hair down made him almost trip over the curb. She'd looked so beautiful with the firelight shimmering in those golden waves. Drake had often dreamed of what it would be like to bury his hands in her hair, to lose himself in her kisses.

"Knock it off!" he groused to himself, drawing the admonishing scowl of Mrs. Beeler as he jogged past her house. The school principal stood in her driveway, attempting to shovel away snow. The woman was a cranky, fusty old thing who didn't care for children. He'd heard rumors she planned to retire at the end of the school year. That would be a good thing for everyone.

He'd jogged halfway down the block before he spun around and returned to her driveway. "Do you need some help, Mrs. Beeler?" he asked, jogging in place as she set down the shovel and leaned on it.

"What will you charge?" she asked, narrowing her gaze at him.

"Nothing," Drake said, wishing he'd kept on running. "No charge."

She straightened and shot him a speculative stare. "This won't earn you any bonus points at school."

"I didn't expect it to," Drake said, taking the shovel from her and going to work on her driveway. Hefting the heavy, wet snow gave him a good work out and burned off some of the energy and unsettled tension that had filled him the past few weeks.

It took him thirty minutes to finish. When he did, Mrs. Beeler came out of her house where she'd retreated to watch his every move from the front window. She handed him a bottle of water with a curt nod. "Thank you, Drake. That was kind of you."

"You know, 'tis the season." He forced a smile as he backed toward the street. "Enjoy the rest of your day, Mrs. Beeler."

After taking a long swig of water, he returned to his run. He drained the bottle and left it in a recycle bin near city hall, looped past the town square and jogged past Rhett's garage. He couldn't help but smile at the tree Rhett had made of stacked tires and decorated with strings of lights. There was also a snowman made of stacked tires painted white with an old hubcap for a hat and wrenches for arms.

He lengthened his stride and headed through town and ran past Rhett's place. Lolly wasn't out in the pasture, so he glanced back at Cedar's house and saw the camel lounging in the yard. That probably wasn't going to earn Rhett any points with the neighbor since she was mad at him anyway.

He ran for a mile, turned around and headed back into Faraday. Drake slowed his pace and looked down Main Street. Lights twinkled through the snow that fell softly in big flakes. Garlands and wreaths adorned businesses, adding to the festive atmosphere. He took a deep breath and smelled wood smoke blending with a distinctive pine scent from the tree lot across the street.

Maybe he and Drew just needed a little holiday cheer.

Drake jogged over to the tree lot and left five minutes later with a small three-foot tall tree that would have made Charlie Brown proud. He carried it home and stamped the snow from his feet before gently shaking it from the tree. When he stepped inside, warmth hit his cold-numbed cheeks, making them sting.

"Thought I might have to go find your frozen carcass and haul it home," Drew teased as he sat on the couch, mindlessly flipping through channels with a postal magazine open upside down on his lap.

"I stopped to help Mrs. Beeler shovel her driveway." Drake kicked off his damp shoes and toed them toward the heating vent to dry.

"That was nice, considering she doesn't even need a costume on Halloween for her annual appearance as a mean, cranky, old witch." Drew rose from the couch and pointed to Drake's tree. "Did you tackle a kid with a head shaped like a bowling ball wearing a yellow and black shirt on your way back here and steal his tree?"

Glad his brother still owned a little bit of his usual humor, Drake grinned and held out the tree. "No bald-headed kids were harmed in the acquisition of this tree, but I thought it might help us find a little Christmas spirit."

"What are we going to decorate it with and where are we going to put it?" Drew asked as he moved into the kitchen and started rummaging through the cupboards to find a container to hold the tree. He held up a big pickle jar they sometimes used to make sun tea in the summer. "Will this work?"

"It should. Fill it with water." Drake took Drew's pocket knife from where he'd left it by the door with his keys and cut off a few straggly little limbs near the bottom of the tree. Drew moved the jar to the small kitchen table. When Drake set the tree in the jar, he and Drew both waited with hands out to see if it would tip, but it held steady.

"Ornaments?" Drew asked, turning to look around the apartment.

"I have an idea," Drake said, grinning at his brother.

An hour later, they were both chuckling as they finished decorating the tree and stepped back to admire their efforts. They started to string popcorn but realized neither of them would survive being poked repeatedly with the needle they tried to jab through the kernels so they abandoned that idea. Instead, they added ornaments of bow-tie pretzels, fishing bobbers and lures, a few small wrenches and screwdrivers, and a handful of candy canes Drew had received from one of his customers the previous day. While Drew dug through their recycle bin and retrieved enough caps off pop bottles to glue them into a star shape, Drake used plain white paper to make a paper chain similar to the one he helped Nick fashion the other evening.

"Not too bad, bro," Drew said, thumping Drake on the back as they surveyed their handiwork.

"It still needs something around the bottom," Drake said, tilting his head to the side.

"I know what to use," Drew said. He disappeared into his bedroom and returned with a pale blue T-shirt. He draped it around the jar. Surprisingly, it looked quite similar to the baby blue blanket Charlie Brown's friend Linus draped around his sad little tree.

"Perfect!" Drake gave his brother a high five.

"Hey, this will be fun for Seth and Rhett to see when they come over Friday," Drew said as he took cheese out of the fridge and started assembling sandwiches for their dinner.

"Is Rhett planning to come?" Drake asked as he dug a can of soup out of the cupboard and dumped it into a microwave-safe bowl. "I know he's still mad at me."

"Nah. I think he's mostly mad at himself for not being up-front with Cedar in the first place." Drew glanced over at him as he added a glob of butter to a frying pan and waited for it to melt before he set in a sandwich. "What about you? You've been acting weird, even for you, bro. What's going on?"

Drake shook his head, unwilling to admit the truth to anyone, including Drew. "Not a thing. Just a lot of stuff happening at school with Christmas and programs, you know."

Drew gave him a long, observant look, but refrained from saying anything as he flipped over the sandwich.

"Did you hear Seth say…"

Grateful for his brother's abrupt change of subject, Drake half-listened as he thought about ways to convince Angela they should be more than friends. Much, much more.

Chapter Seven

"What would you like to do today, baby?" Angela asked as she placed their breakfast dishes in the dishwasher.

Nick hopped down from the counter where he'd been tossing his yo-yo and fisted his little hands at his waist. "Mom! You know I'm going with Sean and Evan today. Remember? You said I could go."

Angela nodded her head as she picked up a dishrag and wiped off the counters and stovetop.

"I'm sorry, Nick. I completely forgot. Yes, you may still go. What time did we agree to go over?" She reached for her phone but Nick grabbed her hand.

"Sean's mommy is going to pick me up. Evan is coming, too. We're going rollerskating and then out for pizza at that fun place by the mall."

Distracted by the holidays and the ache in her heart, and haunted by her past as well as thoughts of Drake, Angela had completely forgotten she'd agreed to allow Nick to go with his friends for a fun day in Portland. Lisa McGregor, Sean's mother, had assured Angela she didn't mind taking the boys and promised to have Nick home in time for dinner when they'd discussed plans earlier in the week.

"It sounds like a great day, honey. You better brush your teeth and comb your hair, and maybe change into a different shirt." Angela watched Nick race off toward his room. She wondered what she could do to properly thank Lisa for taking on three rambunctious boys for the day. The busy mom might appreciate it if she offered to take a turn watching them during Christmas break. Lisa worked at the bank and her husband managed the hardware store. Neither of them would have any extra time off between Christmas and New Year's Day. As long as no emergencies popped up, Angela could take the boys for a day and do something with them. Nick had been begging her to go sledding. She could make a day of it and take all three boys. Maybe Drake would like to go along. He'd certainly make the day more fun.

Stop it! Why did her thoughts always have to wander around to him? *Because he's the best friend you've ever had.* Drake truly was, even if she hadn't been much of a friend to him lately.

The more her attraction to him grew, the more distance she tried to put between them. It wasn't fair to him, especially when she continued to refuse to admit what was bothering her. She was sure he assumed her unusual behavior stemmed from her grief over her grandmother. That was a small part, but not all of it.

Angela tossed the dishrag into the sink then rinsed her hands and dried them. A glance at the clock confirmed Lisa would be there soon. "Are you ready, Nick?"

"Coming, Mom!" Nick yelled before his footsteps thudded down the hallway. He raced into the living room with his hair slicked down and his face shining, both from a scrubbing and the excitement he couldn't contain. He'd changed into a dark blue sweatshirt with Captain America's shield screen-printed on the front and a hint of gray from a T-shirt beneath it peeked around the collar.

"What T-shirt did you pick?" Angela asked, lifting her purse and digging around for her wallet.

Nick gave her a quelling look and sighed. "Captain America, Mom."

"Of course. How did I not know that?" she asked with a hint of sarcasm. She took money from her wallet and folded it up then stuffed it in Nick's front jeans' pocket. Before he could protest, she put a dab of glue in the pocket and held it closed with one hand while the other circled around his back.

"Mom! What are you doing?" Nick tried to squirm free, but she held him steady.

"I don't want you to lose the money. The glue will keep it from falling out of your pocket, but if you need it, you can get to it easily enough. Don't have an attack, Nick."

The little boy huffed. "Just don't glue it to my underwear. One time Timmy Irwin came to school and his mom pinned a note in his pocket, but she got the pin in his underwear and he had an accident 'cause he couldn't get the pin off."

Angela shook her head. "That must have been terrible for Timmy. I promise, the glue is just in your pocket." She glanced up at Nick and forced herself not to run a hand through the hair he'd carefully combed. Her baby was growing up too fast. "Do you promise to mind Mrs. McGregor?"

Nick rolled his eyes. "Yes, Mom. And not be loud in the car or mess around with Sean and Evan when we're supposed to be good. I'll pay attention when we cross the street and…" Nick rubbed a finger alongside his nose and squinted his eyes, trying to remember all the rules Angela worked so hard to instill in him. "Oh, and I'll say please and thank you."

"Very good, baby." Angela gave Nick a hug and kissed his cheek. "I hope you have a great time today."

"I know I will, Mom. It's always fun when I get to go to Portland, but I like Faraday, too. Not everywhere has a camel. I'm excited Shep gets to be the sheep in the nativity again this year. Miss Cooke is going to let her donkey be in it, too. Will Lolly like Pete? Lolly likes Shep. Will Mr. Stafford bring his cow again? I like the fuzzy red and white ones best."

"I'm sure there will be plenty of animals at the nativity. It's a few weeks away, anyway." Angela retrieved Nick's good coat and made sure he had gloves and a stocking cap as well as a few tissues in the pockets. "Are you ready to tell me what you want for Christmas, Nick?"

Stubbornly, her son shook his head. "Santa is going to bring it. That's the only, only thing I want this year. You don't have to get me anything, Mommy. But a Christmas tree would be good."

"I promise I'll get a tree before Christmas Eve, Nick." Angela held back a sigh. After setting out most of the decorations, Angela hadn't been able to open the special box of Granny's decorations. She just couldn't handle the pain and memories right now. The same feelings would surface the moment she opened the box of ornaments for the tree since Granny had made most of them.

Nope. Angela wanted to put off that painful job as long as possible, no matter how much Nick wanted a tree up and decorated.

"There's Mrs. McGregor," Nick said, snatching his coat from her hands and racing toward the door.

Angela grabbed a few more bills from her wallet and followed him outside.

"Hi, Lisa!" Angela waved as the woman got out of her minivan and walked around to greet them.

"Hey, Angela. You have fun plans today?" Lisa asked as she pushed open the door and Sean and Evan looked out, talking excitedly to Nick.

"Not yet. Are you sure you want to do this?"

Angela asked as the boys chattered and laughed while she fastened in Nick's booster seat.

Lisa smiled. "I don't mind at all. I figure while they're skating I can knock out getting my Christmas cards ready to mail. We should be back around four."

"That'll be perfect. If I have an emergency call and won't be here, I'll send you a text." Angela said, giving Nick a hug as he remembered to tell her goodbye. She bent down to kiss him, but he squirmed away and climbed in the van with his friends.

Lisa exchanged a knowing look with her. "They get so big so fast."

"That they do." Angela watched as Lisa shut the door. "I appreciate you giving me a day to myself. I'd like to return the favor. Maybe after Christmas?"

"That would be fantastic. Kevin and I will both be working that week so I've yet to figure out what to do with Sean while school's out." Lisa gave Angela a quick hug. "Just tell me when and he'll be here."

Angela smiled. "I'll pick a day for sure and let you know." She handed Lisa the money she'd brought out with her. "Take this for Nick's skating admission, and lunch, and snacks, and whatever else pops up today."

Lisa tried to hand the money back to her, but Angela shook her head. "That boy will eat more than his share, so please keep it."

"Fine, but only if I can do the same when you take Sean," Lisa said.

"Fair enough." Angela stepped back from the van. "At least the weather is cooperating today. It isn't supposed to snow until tomorrow evening."

"I know. If the roads were bad this morning, the boys would be out of luck because there is no way I'm driving down or up the mountain when it's snowing." Lisa climbed behind the wheel and shut the door.

"Have a great day!" Angela called and waved before she moved back to the front porch. She watched until the van turned onto the main road then went back inside.

She hadn't spent a day alone without work or responsibilities pressing down on her since before Nick was born.

For a few minutes, she stood in the living room and looked around, as though she was seeing the house for the first time. It really was a nice home, sturdy and well-built. Angela had purchased a new couch when they moved to Faraday, but the other pieces were things that had once belonged to her grandmother.

The room was a blend of old and new, traditional and modern. Angela smiled. The living room reflected how she so often felt, a blending of past and present. She just needed to let a dash of hope for the future trickle in.

Then again, that kind of thinking led her straight back to Drake and how much she loved him, wanted to be loved by him. The man clearly saw her as a friend, nothing more. Perhaps he never would return her romantic feelings.

Her phone chimed, so she took it from her

pocket and grinned as his name popped up on the screen.

"Hey, what's up?" she asked as she answered the call.

"Last time I checked, the sky, along with inflation, and maybe the power bill."

Angela shook her head at Drake's teasing. "Seriously, Drake. What's going on?"

"A little birdie told me you are footloose and fancy free today. I'm curious if you have plans."

Angela wondered who had told Drake that Nick was going to spend the day with his friends. It could have been Nick at school, or one of the many members of the local galloping gossipers. She'd quickly learned life in the tiny town could sometimes be like living in a glass fishbowl where everyone knew everything within five minutes of it happening.

"Angela?" Drake asked, pulling her from her thoughts.

"I'm here. Sorry. Yes, Nick went with Sean and Evan today. He is super excited about rollerskating and pizza."

Drake chuckled. "I can imagine. The boys were talking about it all day yesterday. I think they even planned to wear matching shirts."

"Nick had his Captain America shirt and sweatshirt on when they left. "Angela grinned. "So, to answer your question, I have no plans because, bad mother that I am, I forgot all about him being gone today."

"You aren't a bad mother, Angela. Nick is a very lucky boy to have you. Believe me, I know. I see parents every day and a few truly are bad. You are miles away from that title, my friend."

She heard what sounded like a car door shut then her doorbell rang. Maybe Lisa had already endured all she could handle with three rascally boys and was already back with Nick. "Hang on, Drake. Someone is at the door."

Angela crossed the living room and pulled open the door to find Drake standing there, leaning against the doorjamb wearing a big smile.

"Hey, Angel." The combination of his deep voice and him calling her Angel made her knees quiver.

"Hey, yourself. What are you doing here?" she asked, stepping aside so he could enter as she stuffed her phone inside her pocket.

"I've heard you mention a few times that you used to love to ski." Drake grinned and pointed out the window toward the mountain visible through the frosty-edged glass. "And there's that beautiful mountain with six inches of fresh powder, just begging for us to take advantage of it. Come on, it'll be fun." Drake crossed his arms over his chest. "I'm not taking no for an answer unless you can present a compelling argument."

"But I… you know I… What if…" Angela couldn't think up an excuse, especially with Drake standing in front of her looking like he stepped out of a photo shoot for an outdoor clothing company. His hair was tussled, not combed and moussed in an upward swoop like he wore it for school. He had on a pair of navy ski pants with a navy and teal ski jacket. The jacket was open, revealing a form fitting cream-colored thermal shirt that outlined every muscle of his lean, trim form.

Her mouth went dry and she raised her gaze to his. The colors of the jacket made his eyes even bluer. Mesmerized, she backed away from him, unable to process a single thought except one — she couldn't pass up the opportunity to spend the day with Drake. Not when he stood like a gift-wrapped present in her living room.

He grinned. "Can't think of a reason not to go, can you?"

"Well, no. Not at the moment," she admitted.

Drake turned her around and gave her a slight nudge forward. "Get on your ski duds, lady. I'm taking you to the slopes."

"But, Drake. What if…"

"Go!" He gave her another nudge. "While you change, do I need to feed your critters or anything?"

"No, everyone already had their breakfast." Angela glanced back at him before she went into her bedroom. "If you're hungry, there are a few leftover chocolate chip muffins on the counter."

"Thanks. I'll just help myself."

Angela shut her bedroom door and yanked off the baggy sweatshirt and yoga pants she'd pulled on earlier that morning.

She tugged on a pair of moisture-wicking thermal pants with a matching shirt then exchanged her fuzzy socks for a pair of heavy wool socks. After a few minutes of digging in the back of her closet, she unearthed a pair of ski pants from years ago and pulled them on, hoping they'd fit. They were a little snug, but not uncomfortably so.

She hurried into the bathroom and jerked out the few pins holding up her messy bun then combed her hair into a ponytail. After brushing her teeth, she nearly poked her eye out as she hastily applied mascara. Before she left the bathroom, she dabbed a bit of perfume behind her ears and on her wrists, then wished she hadn't. She didn't want to give Drake the wrong impression. Today was about two friends hanging out and having a good time. Wasn't it?

"Friends, friends, friends," she chanted quietly as she dug out a long scarf and grabbed a sweatshirt that zipped up the front as well as her ski jacket. She no longer had her skis, goggles or ski boots, but she supposed all the equipment could be rented when they reached the slopes.

"I'm ready to go," she said, stepping into the kitchen. She tossed the sweatshirt, jacket, and scarf on the counter then reached back to pull the band in her ponytail tighter.

Drake's gaze zeroed in on her and he choked on the drink of milk he'd just swallowed. He set down the glass and thumped his chest with his fist then turned his face away and coughed.

"Are you okay?" she asked, hurrying over and patting him on the back.

"Great," he wheezed. "Never better."

She grinned and moved back. "You are a horrible liar, Drake Miller. Did you inhale some muffin crumbs down the wrong pipe or something?"

"Something," he rasped and drained the milk in his glass then filled it half full of water and chugged it down before he turned to face her.

Angela pulled on the sweatshirt and went to find a pair of gloves in the basket she kept by the back door. She gathered a few essential items from her purse and stowed her phone, wallet, lip balm and gum in her assorted pockets. The mother in her grabbed a few tissues and she stuffed them into her coat pocket then she turned to Drake. "Are you ready to go?"

"Yes, ma'am, I am."

He held open the front door for her then followed her out to his SUV. When she reached for the passenger door, he hurried to open it before she could then offered her a gallant bow. "Your carriage awaits, milady."

"Thank you, kind sir." She took his hand, ignoring the flurry of sensations that erupted from the point of contact and shot up her arm as she climbed inside his vehicle.

Electric. His touch felt positively electric. Maybe she should feign a sudden headache and run back inside the safety of her house.

Drake slid behind the wheel and shot her a rakish grin. "You aren't baling on me now, Angel. We are doing this."

Surprised he could read her thoughts so easily, she hoped he hadn't figured out how enthralled she was with him. If that was the case, he'd probably shove her out the door and never return.

"When was the last time you skied?" Drake asked as they drove up the highway that would take them to the slopes on Mount Hood.

"Oh, gosh, I guess it would have been almost

eight years ago." Angela looked outside, awed by the rugged beauty of the landscape. Snow-frosted trees on either side of the road almost looked ethereal in the gilded morning light. "You'll have to let me practice on the kiddie slopes first."

Drake laughed. "I haven't been for a while, either. Drew and I used to go all the time, but life gets busy."

"It surely does." Angela looked over at him. "So how are things going with Drew and Joy?"

"I think Drew and Joy are the only two who don't see how perfect they are for each other," Drake said, shaking his head. "My brother is so dense, I'm not sure he'll ever figure it out. He was moping around last week and didn't spend time with her, but he said he planned to go to her place after work today, so maybe that's progress."

"She seems like a wonderful person, Drake. In fact, I keep meaning to go over and see her again. I'm sure it's hard being stuck in the house like she is until her injury heals. Winter is the worst time to have a foot or leg injury."

"I know. Seth's grandpa is stuck at home, too. I swear, this snow we've had has left a lot of people in bad situations."

Angela nodded. "It's hard on the animals, too."

Drake glanced at Angela. "Seth said you stopped by one day when they almost lost a calf. Ivy is Sam's special bovine, so that would have been tragic."

"Ivy throws awesome calves, though." Angela smiled. "And I met Sam's nurse."

Drake's eyebrow lifted. "What did you think of

her? I've heard varying reports."

Angela laughed. "She's gorgeous and full of fun, so if Seth told you anything else, he's fibbing."

A smirk made the dimple in Drake's chin pop out. "And here I thought she had fangs and claws."

The tension melted away and the two of them visited like old friends on the rest of the drive. After Drake parked, they made their way to the ski rental shop where they both rented skis, boots, and Angela got a pair of goggles.

"Remember, I'm going to be rusty," she said after she strapped on the skis and stood. "Be gentle with me."

Although she meant the comment in a teasing manner, Drake cupped her chin in his hand and gave her a look full of such emotion, it momentarily stunned her. "Always, Angel. I'd never be anything else."

In an abrupt switch, he grabbed her hand and motioned to the ski lift. "Come on, my little ski bunny. Let's hit the slopes."

An hour later, Angela laughed as she and Drake stopped at the bottom of a slope. It hadn't taken long for her body and mind to remember how to ski. When she stopped trying to think about how to ski and just did it, she had no problem keeping up with Drake.

"I thought you said you were rusty," he said, grinning as they removed their goggles and looked back up at the slope they'd just skied down.

"I am. Can't you tell?" she cast him a flirty glance over her shoulder as she headed toward the ski lift.

"No, I can't."

"I'll race you down, slow poke."

They ate a picnic lunch from a basket of sandwiches, fruit, and cookies Drake's mother had packed for them. She'd just brushed the last cookie crumbs from her fingers when Drake talked her into trying snowboarding. After turning in their skis, they rented the necessary equipment and headed back out.

Angela had a blast and laughed every time she or Drake took a spill. Once, they fell almost on top of each other.

"Are you okay?" Drake asked, raising himself up and staring into her face, searching for something she hesitated to define.

"I'm great, Drake," she said, smiling up at him. Desperate to wrap her arms around his neck and pull him down for a kiss, she clenched her hands at her sides to keep from putting her thoughts into actions.

"Angela," he whispered, his gloved hand cupping her cheek. "Sweet Angel..." His head started to dip toward hers. Afraid he was going to kiss her and terrified he wouldn't, she grabbed a handful of snow and tossed it in his face.

Startled, he pulled back, spitting snow. "You are so in for it, young lady. Just you wait. I'll get you back when you least expect it." Drake rose and pulled her to her feet as she laughed at him.

"I'm two years older than you, so you can't go around calling me young lady."

Drake fished snow from inside his coat collar. "I can call you anything I want when you bombard me with snow."

They played on the slopes until they both noticed it starting to get dark.

Angela cast a panicked glance at the sky, and then grabbed her phone from her pocket. "Oh, my gosh, Drake! It's almost four. Lisa said she'd bring Nick home at four. Even if we hurry, we won't make it in time." She took off at a jog, carrying her phone in one hand and the snowboard in the other. "Ugh, and Lisa left three messages. How did I miss them?"

"Not to worry," Drake said, catching up to her in a few long strides. He wrapped an arm around her shoulders as they made their way toward the equipment rental shop. "Lisa is going to leave Nick at the café with my folks. After dinner, Drew is going to take him over to Joy's place to play with Bacon and Pete."

Angela scowled at him and pushed away from his side. "That is not okay, Drake. Not at all. Who gave you permission to decide anything about my son?"

Drake stepped back from her and frowned. "Honestly, Angela? You were having such a good time today I didn't want you to feel rushed to get back to Faraday. I kept an eye on the clock and when I knew we wouldn't be back in time to meet Nick at your house, I made other arrangements. My apologies if I overstepped. If you want to leave, I'll take you home right now."

"As a matter of fact I do." They left the equipment at the shop then walked to the parking lot in silence. Angela listened to a voice mail message from Lisa letting her know the boys were having a great time and they would be home at four. The second message assured her she was happy to leave Nick at the café and she hoped Angela enjoyed her afternoon on the slopes. A text message told her she supposed she should have checked to make sure it was okay to leave Nick with the Millers at the café. If it was a problem, she just needed to let Lisa know.

Angela yanked off her gloves and shoved them in a pocket then quickly texted Lisa letting her know it was fine to leave Nick at the café and thanking her for taking him for the day. When she finished, she glanced up at Drake and tucked her phone in her pocket.

He looked miserable, like a little boy who'd gotten in trouble for sneaking a cookie right before dinner. When Drake opened the passenger door to his SUV, Angela squeezed his hand. "I'm not used to having anyone help with Nick and I'm really, really not used to having a day to enjoy myself. I'm sorry if I snapped at you, but going forward, please don't make plans for Nick without consulting me. I do appreciate the arrangements you made for him this evening, though. He'll have a great time with your folks, and with Drew and Joy. I just don't want to inconvenience anyone."

"Are you kidding?" Drake gave her a hand inside then jogged around the front of the SUV and slid behind the wheel. "My mom is pumped that Nick will be there for dinner and Drew said Joy was thrilled he's coming over. The puppy will have a great time playing with someone closer to his size."

Angela's phone chimed and she pulled it out, hiding a grin as she read Lisa's text.

Enjoy yourself with that handsome bachelor on the slopes. Milk it for all it's worth, girl!

"So what's next?" Angela asked, as she texted a winking emoji face to Lisa then tucked the phone back in her pocket.

"Next?" Drake gave her a questioning look as he pulled out of the parking lot onto the road. "You mean you aren't in a rush to go home?"

"Well, since you've already gone to all the effort of making arrangements for Nick and I've gotten over my initial tizzy fit about it, I'm not in a hurry. Besides, Nick is probably already at the café and I'd hate to disappoint him or your mom." Angela grinned at him. "Assuming you had further plans for the evening in mind."

Chapter Eight

Drake cleared his throat. Boy, did he have other plans in mind, but Angela wouldn't like a single one of them. Not when they started with kissing her and ended with... kissing her.

All day, he'd battled to keep his feelings in check even if his thoughts ran rampant. Multiple times, he'd almost kissed the beguiling beauty sitting beside him, but he'd managed to resist. Barely. The one time he'd almost surrendered to the temptation, she'd tossed snow in his face. It might have chilled the moment, but did nothing to cool his ever-growing ardor for the woman.

He loved her. Wanted her. But how in the world could he convince her to see him as something beyond a friend?

The day had been amazing and good for them both, but then he had to go taking charge, like he was often inclined to do, and make her upset. Angry, even.

She'd looked like an enraged mama bear when she dressed him down for making plans without consulting her. If Drake was easily frightened, that would have done the trick. Only he deserved her wrath. Looking back, he should have told her at the time, suggested his plan, and let her decide what she wanted to do.

However, Drake had forged ahead without asking her opinion because he'd wanted to keep her to himself longer. Given the option of going home to Nick or staying with him, Drake knew she'd rush back to Faraday. Part of him, that stupid ego part, took a hit knowing that she'd always put Nick first. The sensible part of him cheered Angela for being an awesome parent. He admired her dedication to her son.

Through his years of teaching he'd watched enough people to know parenting a child was hard. Being a single parent was incredibly challenging. And balancing being a single parent with a hectic career was close to impossible, but somehow Angela succeeded.

Nick was a happy kid who rarely misbehaved or got into trouble while seeking attention. The little boy was a normal, inquisitive, bright student who loved his mom.

Drake was definitely a card-carrying member of Angela's fan club. He just didn't think she was ready to hear him admit it. Not yet. Maybe not ever.

Today, though, he wouldn't worry about the future and what might happen, or not, between the two of them. For now, he'd be content that he had several more hours to spend with Angela and enjoy each and every one.

He pulled into the parking lot at the ski lodge and into one of the few open spaces. "Hungry?" he asked as he unfastened his seatbelt.

"Famished. I can't believe I'm hungry after eating that great lunch your mom packed." Angela unfastened her seatbelt, but Drake hurried around to open her door before she could get out.

He gave her his hand and she took it as she hopped out of the SUV. Rather than relinquish it, he held on, rocked by the jolt that shot up his arm each time they touched. Could she really not feel it?

"Are you sure we're dressed appropriately for the lodge? Isn't it fancy in there?" Angela asked as they neared the door.

"You look perfect. Perfect and beautiful," Drake assured her then pulled open the door and they stepped inside. For the first time since he'd met her, Angela appeared carefree and full of youthful zest. He loved seeing this side of her, loved watching her long golden waves of hair bob in the ponytail at the back of her head, loved watching her smile and listening to her laugh. Her laugh wasn't one of those annoying high-pitched screeches or mindless little girl-like giggles. It was rich and warm and made Drake want to do whatever he could to draw out more of it.

Inside, Angela came to a stop as she stared at the two-story rock fireplace flanked by towering Christmas trees. "Oh, wow." She turned in a slow circle, taking in the architectural details of the historic resort.

Drake remained silent as she looked around then placed his hand at the small of her back and guided her to the restaurant where he gave the hostess his name.

"You made a reservation?" Angela whispered as they followed the hostess to a table. "That's a bold move, Miller."

He grinned and held her chair for her as she took a seat. "Hopeful. It was a hopeful move that you'd agree to have dinner with me."

"Whatever," she smiled as the hostess handed her a menu. She glanced through it then looked at Drake. "I take it you've eaten here before. What's good?"

"Everything." Drake smirked as he set down the menu and fought the urge to move so he sat next to Angela instead of across the table.

Angela perused the menu then sat back and took a sip from her glass of water. "Tell me about this place," she said, waving her hand toward the massive rock chimney.

Their seats in the second-story restaurant put them in a wonderful position to see the fireplace and also look out the window at the lights and softly falling snow. With candlelight flickering on their table, Drake thought it might just qualify as a romantic atmosphere.

He nodded and gazed down at the grouping of furniture in front of the fireplace where people gathered and laughed. "The lodge was built back in the 1930s by the WPA."

"That's the Works Progress Administration, right?" Angela asked, leaning slightly forward on the table.

"Yep, that's right."

A smiling server appeared and took their orders. When she left, Drake pointed to the area below them. "The workers who built the lodge added a lot of unique details, like hand carving every newel post. The lodge was dedicated by President Roosevelt. It's a national historic landmark and, following the tradition from when it first opened, there are St. Bernard dogs that are kind of the mascots of the lodge."

"That is awesome," Angela said, gazing downstairs then looking back at Drake. She reached across the table and placed her hand over his where it fiddled with his fork in nervous agitation. "Thank you for bringing me here. This is the first time I've had a lovely dinner out in almost ten years."

"That's too long, Angela." Drake gave her a studying glance then lifted her hand to his lips and kissed the back of it. He saw something flicker in the chocolate-depths of her eyes, something that looked a lot like yearning and a little like love. "Do you mind my asking what happened to your husband? All you've ever said is that he died before Nick was born."

She pulled her hand away and fell silent as she stared outside. Drake wished he'd kept silent. They were having such a good time together and he had to bumble ahead and ruin it.

"It's okay, Angela. You don't have to tell me."

She turned from the window and offered him a sad, resigned look. "No, Drake. You're my best friend and it's time I told you the whole story, but it's not for the faint of heart."

"I've got a pretty tough one," he teased, slapping a hand to his chest then doing his best to look encouraging. "I can take it."

Angela nodded and settled her hands in her lap. "My grandparents lived on a farm near a small town in Tennessee. Actually, Faraday reminds me of it quite a bit. They had one son, my father. Although my grandfather hoped he'd stay on the farm, my dad hated it. All he could think about was getting away and moving to a big city. Granny and Papa didn't have a lot of money, so my dad kept his grades up and worked hard. When he was sixteen, Papa died at a neighbor's place. He was helping fix a tractor and it rolled over him. Granny says losing Papa made my dad that much more desperate to leave. And he started drinking. Dad earned an engineering scholarship to a college in Denver where he met my mother. Right after he graduated, they wed and he went to work for a great company. A few years later, they had me. My mother lives in a state of denial about life in general and my dad in particular. During the day, he's a respected engineer, but once he gets home, he drinks. Sometimes he's verbally abusive, although I've never known him to be physically violent. To their credit, they sent me to stay with Granny anytime I had a break from school. Those were the happiest moments of my childhood, when I was with her at the little farm in Tennessee."

Drake didn't know what to say and sensed Angela just needed to share the whole story without interruption, so he remained silent.

She took a sip of water, toying with the stem of the glass before releasing a pain-infused sigh. "When I was a sophomore in college, I met a senior who was about to graduate with a degree in software engineering. His name was Allen Plankton. He was charming and good-looking, said all the right things. He and my mother seemed to really hit it off. She told me over and over I would never do better than Allen. So when he proposed, I said yes. After all the years of my father telling me how I wasn't good enough or smart enough, Allen was full of flattery. He made me feel smart and beautiful, like I could do anything. We wed right before I started my senior year of college. Within a month, I knew I'd made a huge mistake. Allen had gone from being sweet and charming to possessive and cruel. Constantly, he'd check up on me, wanting to know where I was and what I was doing. For reasons I'll never understand, he was convinced I was cheating on him. If I wasn't in class or at my part-time job on campus, he wanted me right beside him. He'd randomly show up at school, following me. Every day became a battle of wills. Although I was against it, he and my mother insisted we move into a little apartment above my parents' garage to save money, since vet school was expensive. I had scholarships and he earned good money at his job, so it wasn't like we couldn't manage, but he and my mother wouldn't relent."

"Your mother?" Drake asked.

Angela nodded. "Allen had Mom completely fooled. She always sided with him, told me I should drop out of the vet program and be a devoted wife. I was in my last year of school when I found out he'd put a tracking app on my phone, hacked into my lab computer, and spent more time stalking me than he did at his job. I freaked and kicked him out of the apartment. Mom invited him to live in the house with her and Dad."

Drake watched as Angela started trembling. She started to lift the glass of water then set it down before she dropped it. He captured her hand between both of his. "Hey, it's okay, Angel. You don't have to say any more."

"I need to tell you, Drake. I need to just get it out in the open. I've never told anyone but my Granny the whole story." Angela took a deep breath. "One night, after Allen and Dad had been drinking, he came to the apartment. Mom had given him a key. He um... he attacked me. At my mother's urging, he moved back into the apartment. I tried to hide from him, to stay with friends, but he'd always find me. I sometimes wonder if he hadn't somehow installed a tracking device on my car. He grew abusive, violent. Then I realized I was pregnant in spite of staying on birth control pills. There was no way I wanted Allen or my parents in my baby's life, so I started making plans to leave, to escape. I was only a month away from finishing my degree. After that, I could disappear and start over. Allen somehow figured out my plans and confronted me. He hit me until I passed out then set the apartment on fire. The sound of flames crackling and glass exploding woke me. I managed to climb out the bedroom window onto the top of the garden shed and made it to the neighbor's house to call for help."

A tear rolled down her cheek and Drake reached over to brush it away. Her eyes held such a look of desolation, it made him wish he could take away the pain she'd endured.

"I don't know if Allen was so drunk he didn't know what he was doing or if he had a change of heart, but he went back into the apartment and burned to death. My mother blamed me for everything and my father... well, he dealt with the situation by pouring a few extra drinks. I spent a week in the hospital recovering from my injuries, but miraculously, I didn't lose the baby. Despite everything, I wanted my child. So, I finished my classes, graduated with honors, and left the next day for Tennessee. Granny took me in while I put my life back together. After Nick was born, I went to work in a big vet clinic an hour away. Granny was the one who told me it was time to spread my wings and try something new when I told her about the clinic here in Faraday. I just wish she would have made the move with us, but she refused to leave the home she'd known since she was a young bride of eighteen."

"Angel, I'm so, so sorry for what you endured,

what your family put you through. I don't even know what to say. I've always admired you, but that's just increased tenfold. What you went through was horrific, and yet you've remained a wonderful, caring, sweet person who is raising a terrific son."

Visibly shaken, she blinked and brushed at her tears. "Thank you, Drake. And thanks for listening to my story and not bolting out of here."

He gave her a lopsided grin and took her hand in his again, pressing it to his lips. "Never. It'll take more than that to send me running."

The server appeared with their meals and Drake tried to still the hundred questions racing through his thoughts. Before he could stop it, one popped out. "Do you stay in contact with your folks? I've never heard you mention them, other than to say they live in Colorado."

She shook her head and toyed with the pasta on her plate. "No. They don't know about Nick. The only time I've spoken to them since I left Denver was when I called to tell them Granny passed away. Mom made some excuse about being too busy to attend the funeral. She never even asked how I was doing or where I was living." She shrugged. "It's for the best."

"That's their loss, Angel. Besides, you've got a huge family right here."

"I do?" she asked, glancing at him in confusion.

"Are you kidding me? Everyone in town loves you. Well, with the exception of that dog you fixed last week."

Angela grinned as he knew she would.

"I'm serious, Angela. You've made a home and a life for yourself here. You've got more friends than you realize. Friends who would do anything for you."

Her face softened and Drake didn't think she'd ever looked lovelier. "Like you?"

"Like me."

When they finished their entrees, Drake insisted they order dessert. While they waited for it to arrive, they watched the snow falling and looked at the lights outside the window. Suddenly, he felt Angela's finger touch the dimple in his chin. "Granny always said those dimples were made by angel kisses when babies were born."

Drake grinned, liking the idea of his Angel planting a few kisses there, especially if they roamed upward to his lips. "Your granny was a very smart woman."

"You have no idea."

While they lingered over dessert and cups of spicy tea, Drake changed the subject to the Christmas season. They talked about the program coming up at school, the community tree lighting, and the living nativity.

"Nick is excited about Shep being in the nativity again," Drake commented as they made their way out to his SUV. The snowfall was heavier, but a snowplow drove by, giving him hope the roads wouldn't be too bad driving back to Faraday.

"He is excited." Angela agreed. "That boy of mine loves Christmas, although I can't get him to tell me what he wants this year. He just keeps saying that Santa is going to bring it and it will be the best Christmas ever."

"Maybe I can try to get it out of him at school or eavesdrop while he's talking to Sean and Evan." Drake smiled at her and waggled an eyebrow. "I have my ways of finding out things."

She laughed. "That would be a huge help. Nick doesn't ask for a lot, so if there is one thing he really wants for Christmas, I'd love to make his wish come true if I can."

"We'll figure it out. After all, it's two adults against a six-year-old. How tough can it be?"

When they reached town, Drake slowly drove down Main Street so they could take in the sight of the holiday decorations before he turned onto the dead-end street where Joy lived.

Together, he and Angela made their way down the walk and to the front door. Angela rang the bell and the sound of giggles, happy barks, and footsteps grew louder then Drew opened the door with Nick and Bacon racing up behind him.

"Hey. How's it going?" Drew asked, stepping back so they could walk inside.

"Mom! I had the best time!" Nick threw his arms around Angela and gave her a hug before he took her hand and tugged her down the hall to the family room where Joy rested on the couch with her leg up. "Miss Joy let me play with Pete and I fed him a carrot, and Mr. Drew, he said I could call him Mr. Drew because Mr. Miller my teacher is Mr. Miller, too. Anyway, Mom, he helped me build a snowman and then we made hot chocolate and watched Rudolph on TV, and Bacon and I played tag and we had cookies. And guess, what, Mom!"

Angela bent down and smiled at her son. "I'll never guess, so you better tell me."

Nick smiled and pointed to a missing space in his bottom row of teeth. "I lost my first tooth today. Miss Joy said the tooth fairy will come visit me and she put my tooth in a box."

Angela dropped to her knees and tipped Nick's face up toward the light so she could examine the hole where his tooth used to be. "I knew it was loose, but I didn't think he'd lose it this soon."

Drew walked over to an end table and picked up a small tin, the kind that mints come in, and handed it to Angela.

Drake moved beside her as she opened the lid and looked down at the little tooth resting on a piece of cotton batting.

"Way to go, buddy!" Drake said, giving Nick a high five. "You've had quite a day."

"It's been the best day I've ever had!" Nick said excitedly, flopping down on the floor and giggling as Bacon licked his cheeks and chin.

Something shifted in Angela, something Drake couldn't define, but wasn't sure he liked. He saw her stiffen as she tucked the tin with Nick's tooth in her pocket. The smile she gave Drew and Joy seemed not as bright as the one she'd worn when they arrived. "I can't thank you enough for this, and for keeping an eye on Nick. Truly, I appreciate it so much."

"Not a problem," Drew said, reaching out and ruffling Nick's hair. The boy jumped up and leaned against his leg as the puppy playfully tugged on his shirttail. "It was fun to hang out with him."

"It really was, Angela. Call anytime you need a babysitter. I'm not very mobile, but Nick minds well. And he had a great time with Pete and Bacon." Joy smiled at her from her place on the couch.

Angela nodded her thanks then pulled Nick to her, as though she needed to reassure herself he was fine. "I better get him home. It's close to bedtime and as wound up as he is, that might take a while."

Drew followed them out to the front porch and waved as Angela fastened Nick's booster seat in the backseat then climbed in beside her son while Drake drove them home.

Disturbed by the fact she'd subtly shifted him into the role of chauffeur, Drake wasn't surprised when she bailed out of the backseat as soon as he stopped in front of her house and pulled Nick along behind her.

"Thanks for a great day, Drake. I'll talk to you later." She shut the door and tugged Nick into the house, shutting Drake out.

He feared it was more than just outside of her home. The look in her eye said it was out of life and heart, too.

Chapter Nine

Drake stood from his desk as the morning bell rang and the last student hurried inside his classroom. The closer it drew to Christmas, the harder it was to get the kids to settle down and study.

Combined with the fact his heart wasn't in the holiday or teaching at the moment, Drake was half inclined to let them have a day just to read, do crafts, and enjoy a long recess… or four. But he'd never once done that in all his years of teaching and he wouldn't start now.

No matter how many knots Angela had twisted in his gut, he couldn't let his students suffer because of it.

The woman had been completely infuriating since the night he drove her home after their day of skiing. He wasn't sure if it was the fact she'd finally shared her past with him or if some overriding guilt about missing the moment when Nick lost his first tooth was the cause, but she'd not only shoved him an arm's length away, she'd reinforced the vast space with a spike-encased brick wall.

Every effort he made to talk to her, to reassure her that nothing she'd said about her parents or husband had changed his feelings for her, ended with him angry and hurt. She'd practically run away from him at the tree lighting ceremony last week and she'd avoided him at church Sunday like he carried five different varieties of the plague.

If she wouldn't even talk to him, how was he supposed to finally work up the nerve to confess he loved her to the very depths of his soul?

He scoffed at himself. If he loved her that much, he wouldn't be sulking in front of a bunch of first-graders instead of figuring out a way to scale her impenetrable walls and claim her heart.

A brief, fleeting moment on Saturday, when he'd almost kissed her, was the one thing giving him hope. A flicker in her eyes, a look on her face, gave him a glimpse into her heart and what he saw there was love. Not love between good friends, although that was there, too.

No, this was the passionate, die-for-you kind of

love that he'd been dreaming of since the first day he met her. Just when he thought he was making progress, when he was certain she was ready to take that next step beyond friendship, she shut him out and locked the door.

Drake forked a hand through his hair and some of the students giggled. He'd forgotten about the mousse he put in it. No doubt it was standing straight up on end, even more than usual. The kids got a kick out of his wacky hairstyle, the silly ties he wore, and the fact he'd goof around with them.

Mindful of fifteen little sets of eyes watching his every move, Drake tamped down his frustration and focused on his students. He did well until craft time arrived that afternoon. Generally, once a week a parent came, brought snacks, and stayed for an hour to help with a craft project. It gave Drake a helping hand and provided the parent with an opportunity to interact with their child and the rest of the class before they went home covered in glitter or glue.

Drake had a special project in mind for today and was excited to share it with the students. "Who's ready for craft time?" he asked as he rose from his desk. All of his students shot their hands in the air. "Great! Clear off your desks and get ready for fun!"

With a stack of construction paper in his hand, Drake walked down the rows of desks and let each student choose a color. He'd stuck with white and a variety of blue shades for this particular project. The students were going to love what came next.

The door opened and Jasper took his cooing to

an accelerated level, like he did when Angela stopped in to visit.

Drake spun around and glared at Angela. She stood in the doorway with two food containers in her hands. What luck! He'd forgotten she'd volunteered weeks ago to help today.

"Come on in," he said, hoping his tone didn't sound as gruff to her as it did to him.

"I came for craft day," she said in a quiet voice, as though she had to explain her presence.

Drake clenched his jaw and nodded.

Angela looked around for a place to set the treats and ended up leaving them on Drake's desk. She removed her coat and left it on an empty hook by the door then pushed up the sleeves of the red thermal shirt she wore beneath a pale blue scrub top featuring reindeer and trees.

Nick leaned over the back of his desk chair and waved at his mother. She smiled and waved back then walked over to Drake. "What can I do to help?"

It was on the tip of his tongue to tell her she could stop freezing him out and let him love her, but that would never do, especially not in front of his class. They'd grown so silent, the only sound in the room was the cooing of Jasper and the hum of the computers in the testing station behind his desk.

"If you'll make sure everyone has a piece of paper, I'll get the rest of our project. It's in the kitchen." Drake handed her the papers and left the room then jogged to the kitchen.

"No running in the halls, Mr. Miller," Mrs. Beeler said, frowning at him as she stepped out of her office.

"Yes, ma'am," he said, slowing to a fast walk as he made his way to the cafeteria.

In the kitchen, Martha, Jo, and Bobbi baked cookies for the next day and already had pans of bread rising for breakfast rolls.

"Did you come to get your goop?" Jo asked with a smile.

"I sure did." Drake accepted the bowl of sparkly goo she handed to him.

"Don't make too big of a mess with that," Bobbi warned.

Drake kissed her wrinkled cheek. "Have I ever done anything like that?"

All three women said, "Yes!"

He chuckled and hurried back down the hall. Mrs. Beeler remained standing in her door and he gave her a brisk nod as he passed her before returning to his classroom.

Angela had taken Jasper out of his cage and let the children gather around the table as Jasper played with a ball. She tucked the bird back inside when Drake opened the door and stepped into the room.

"What's that?" Evan asked as Drake carried the bowl to Jasper's table and set it down.

"Our craft project for the day. Do you know what this is?" he asked as he retrieved a stack of disposable bowls from his storage cupboard and put a scoop of the sparkly, oozing mass in each bowl. He glanced at the students. "Does anyone want to guess what it is?"

"Magic marshmallows!" Megan said, bouncing up and down.

"Unicorn guts!" Billy shouted.

"It's snow slug sludge," Sean said, pointing to the bowl. "Like in the summer when you have slugs and they leave a trail of stuff behind, except this is what snow slugs leave. We had big slugs in Mom's flowers last summer. She let me put salt on them and they curled up like this." Sean curled his hands into claws and made a comical face as he pretended to shrivel on the ground and die.

"Those are all great guesses," Drake said, cutting off any more long, drawn out responses. "But this is snow paint. Today, you're going to paint a scene with a snowman on your paper. Then we'll add a hat and eyes, a nose, and buttons. Everyone sit down and push up your sleeves so you don't get paint on them."

Angela helped push up sleeves of those who couldn't get them on their own. She set a little bowl of paint on each student's desk and passed out paintbrushes.

Once Drake had dipped fifteen bowls of the paint, he went to the front of the room and took a sample project he'd made last night from his desk. "This is what we're going to make, class. Any questions?"

"Can we eat the paint?" Billy asked.

"No, Billy. Do not eat the paint." Drake gave the class a stern look. "Repeat after me, 'I will not eat snow paint.'"

The students repeated the words.

"Good. Now, I will tell you that you can stick your hands in it if you want."

Every student stuck their fingers into the bowl.

Some laughed, a few girls squealed. Drake saw Angela dip her hand in the big bowl near Jasper. "Oh, that's cold," she said, grinning with wonder every bit as childlike as that on the faces of his students.

"It's snow paint, Mrs. Carol. It has to be cold," Evan informed her.

"Of course, Evan." She turned and smiled at Drake and he felt his stupid, traitorous heart rapidly thump in response.

"Everyone get painting!" he said then took half the room to help while Angela oversaw the other half.

When they ended up together at the back of a row, she leaned close to him. "This is a great project. It's giving them so many sensory experiences. The cold temperature of the paint, not to mention the way it oozes through their fingers, and the glitter mixed in. On top of all that, it smells like candy canes. What's it made of?"

"Shaving cream, school glue, iridescent glitter, and peppermint extract." Drake caught a whiff of Angela's soft fragrance and forced himself not to take a deep breath of it.

"You did good, Drake. Then again, you always do," she said in a whisper before moving off to help a little boy who had more paint on his hands than his paper.

When the students finished painting their snowmen, Angela and Drake helped the students position hats, eyes, noses and buttons made of construction paper. "Did you cut all these out?" Angela asked as she picked up another hat and handed it to Emily.

"Part of them. Joy and Drew helped with the rest of them. Joy did the hats, which is why they look awesome. I cut out the carrot-shaped noses, and the lumpy circles are all Drew."

Angela laughed. "It was nice of them to help."

Drake nodded. "Joy said she'd help in the classroom once in a while when she regains the ability to walk."

"She'd be a big help and I think the students would love her."

"I do, too." Drake moved off to assist a student trying to stick noses on each side of his snowman's head for ears.

Angela helped write each child's name on the back of the project then they set the papers on an empty shelf to dry. After the children washed their hands, Angela placed a cute reindeer-patterned paper napkin on each desk then opened the containers with treats. One held crackers topped with thin pieces of ham and cheese cut into holiday shapes. The other contained red gelatin cups with a strawberry nestled inside. A dollop of whipping cream on the top made each little cup look like Santa's hat.

"Santa's hat!" Megan chirped, leaning forward on her desk to look in the container.

"Santa's hat! Santa's hat!" the children chanted.

Drake took the meatier snacks and passed them around while Angela gave each student one of the berry treats.

They'd barely finished eating them when the

five-minute bell rang, letting them know school was about to end for the day.

"Great job today, everyone!" Drake said, moving to the front of the room. "Get your coats and bags, and line up at the door.

The students hurried to obey, pulling on warm boots and coats. Angela reminded them to find their hats and gloves.

Drake walked over to the door and pointed to a sign he'd taped to it long ago. "Let's say our hallway poem."

"I keep my hands to myself, I keep my back straight and tall, I look ahead and not behind, so I'm ready for the hall," the students recited.

"That's awesome, class." Drake smiled as the bell rang. He opened the door and turned them loose. "Have a great evening and I'll see you all tomorrow!"

Angela and Nick picked up a few scattered napkins then Nick took the disinfecting wipes from the cupboard and began wiping the desks while Angela grabbed a handful and went to work on knobs and handles.

"You don't have to help," Drake said, closing the door so Jasper could come out of his cage and play.

Angela released the bird. Jasper hopped around, bumping his ball with his head and cooing happily.

"Many hands make light work," she said, smiling at Drake. "Granny used to say that all the time."

Nick sighed. "I miss Granny."

Angela went over to her son and gave him a hug then kissed the top of his head. "I miss her, too, baby."

Nick glanced over at Drake. "Do you have a granny, Mr. Miller?"

"Not now, but I used to. I had two grandmothers and they both lived in Portland. Drew and I used to visit them in the summer sometimes."

"Aw, I'm sorry your grannies are gone, too." Nick ran over and gave Drake a hug. He kept his arms wrapped around Drake's legs and leaned back to look at him. "I'd share mine with you if I could."

"Thanks, buddy. I appreciate that." Drake took the wipe from Nick and tossed it in the garbage can. "You two go on and get out of here. I can finish cleaning up on my own."

"Are you sure, Drake? We don't mind," Angela said, straightening from where she scrubbed a glob of snow paint off the front of one desk.

"I've got it, but thanks for offering." Drake looked at Nick. "Did you get your tree put up yet?"

Nick scowled at his mother and shook his head. "No. Mom still hasn't gotten one for us."

Drake grimaced and glanced at Angela who was shooting daggers at him from her expressive brown eyes. Eyes that he'd so often wanted to fall into. "Sorry," he mouthed.

Her gaze narrowed as she nudged Nick toward the sink. "Wash your hands, baby. I should run by the clinic and check on one of my patients and then we'll head home."

Drake wiped up paint spills as Angela hustled Nick out the door. Before she left, she tossed him a friendly wave.

Had he sensed a bit of thawing in her frosty attitude? Or had he inhaled too many fumes from the snow paint?

"What do you think, Jasper? Should I give this another shot?"

The dove chased his ball and cooed.

"You really are no help, Jasper. None at all."

Chapter Ten

"It's so nice of you to do this, Jenny," Angela said as she dropped Nick off at his friend Evan's house.

"My pleasure. The day of peacefulness I had when Lisa took Evan made me decide it would be good to take a turn," Jenny Banks said as she watched Nick climb into a booster seat in the back of her suburban. "And Lisa and I are more than happy to turn the boys over to you for a day of sledding after Christmas. They'll love it."

"It's the least I can do," Angela said, giving Nick a wave before Jenny shut the door. She turned to the woman and handed her some money. "For Nick's lunch and whatever else. He has money in his jeans' pocket and I hid ten dollars in his inside coat pocket. That should get him through the day."

Jenny laughed. "I should hope so. I'll have the boys back around three or four."

"Sounds great. If you send me a text, I'll come pick up Nick so you don't have to drive over to my place."

"Oh, I'll drop him off. It's no bother and it isn't that far from leaving Sean at his house anyway. Have a great day, Angela."

"I plan to," she said, smiling at the woman as she climbed in her vehicle and shut the door. Angela walked back to her pickup and slid behind the wheel. For the second time that month, she found herself with an unexpected free Saturday.

Thoughts of the last one made her heart ache. She'd had such a fabulous day with Drake. Honestly, she never wanted it to end. Yes, he'd irritated her when he'd made arrangements for Nick without asking her, but he'd apologized and it turned out fine. Somehow, amid the romantic atmosphere of the lodge, he'd managed to do the impossible and coaxed her into sharing her story, the whole story, of her past.

When he didn't jump up from the table and run, she took it as a good sign. Then they'd gone to see Joy and Drew, and pick up Nick. Her son had lost his first tooth, his first tiny little baby tooth, and she'd missed it because she was off cavorting in the snow with a handsome, incredible man.

At first, she'd been devastated at having Nick's tooth handed to her in a little tin box. By the time she had a few hours to mull it over, though, she knew it wasn't the loss of her son's tooth that made her withdraw from Drake. He could have lost it at school or playing with his pets while she was in the house.

No, it wasn't his tooth that made her turn as frosty as a winter witch on Drake. It was her fear of giving her heart, and the control that went along with that choice, to another man.

She'd been on her own for so long, had raised Nick on her own with no one else's interference or opinions, other than her Granny's, that she wasn't sure she could relinquish control.

A wife was supposed to love and obey her husband. Could she do that? Willingly? Could she trust Drake to keep her heart safe? Could she allow him to be the father her little boy so desperately wanted and needed?

She'd trusted a man once and it ended in a fire-filled nightmare. One that still haunted her from time to time. Her feet bore scars from the flames, but it was the scars on her soul that still pained her.

Tangled in a complicated web of questions for which she had no solid answers, she decided she didn't want to go home to her quiet house and brood. She should go get a Christmas tree, but she still wasn't ready to open Granny's box of ornaments and Nick would insist on it the minute a tree came inside their home.

Angela drove down the mountain to the town at

the base that was ten times as big as Faraday, but far, far smaller than Portland. She went to the shopping mall and purchased a few toys for Nick that she'd heard him discussing with Evan and Sean. She picked up things for his stocking, and a gift for Joy and Drew for their wedding. The couple just got engaged, but had already begun planning a Valentine's Day wedding. By then, Joy's brace would be off and she could walk down the aisle.

From what she'd witnessed, she had a feeling there might be a rash of weddings in Faraday's near future. Seth and Holly planned a ceremony at the ranch as soon as Sam could walk her down the aisle. If she didn't miss her guess, Rhett and Cedar would also be diving into the matrimonial pool soon. She didn't think Rhett had proposed, yet, but she had no doubt that Cedar would eagerly agree when he got around to asking.

Angela stopped in front of a display of holiday-themed underwear for men and grinned. She'd heard all about Drew's split pants and the Grinch peeking out the back. Drake had told her how his mom bought them crazy Christmas underwear every year as a joke.

She quickly sent a text to Barbara, Drake's mom, explaining where she was and asking his size. It took less than a minute for the woman to text her back. With a grin, Angela hurried into the store and bought a bright blue pair of briefs for Drake that had a goofy picture of the abominable snowman on the back, like he was waving to someone.

An idea for a gift for Drake struck her, so she visited a few more stores then carried her purchases out to her pickup. She ate lunch at an Italian restaurant then ran by a big grocery store and loaded her cart. She knew she wouldn't have the time or opportunity to come back shopping again before Christmas.

On the drive home, she cranked Christmas carols on the radio and sang along, trying to capture a bit of the holiday spirit.

She unloaded her pickup, put the groceries away, then hid the gifts in the back of her closet before she decided to go into Faraday. The house seemed too quiet with Nick gone. Besides, the box of Christmas decorations sitting beside the couch taunted her.

Five minutes later, she found herself driving toward Joy's house. Drew would be at work, so she thought the woman might enjoy a visit.

She parked and was half way up the walk when she saw Pete peeking over the newly repaired gate in the fence on the side of the yard.

"Hey, Pete. How are you doing, boy?" she asked, walking over and rubbing the donkey on his neck. "You sure gave Joy and Drew a scare the other day."

No one could figure out what spooked the donkey and made him bust down his gate. Even stranger still was the fact he made a beeline for Lolly, as though he knew right where to find the camel. He'd been unharmed, though. Angela had come over as soon as Joy called to tell her what happened and checked him over.

"Are you ready for the nativity, Pete? You've got a very important role, you know."

141

SHANNA HATFIELD

The donkey bobbed his head and gave her a toothy smile.

Angela laughed and gave him another pat then made it back around to the front porch. The door opened before she could ring the bell and Joy greeted her with a smile. Bacon rushed out and ran a circle around her while barking excitedly.

"What brings you by?" Joy asked, pulling the door open wider.

"I thought you might like some company since I know your cuddly love bear is working today," Angela teased.

Joy's cheeks flushed and she grinned. "Drew would die if he heard anyone call him that, even if he is a cuddly love bear." She snapped her fingers at the puppy. "Bacon, get back in here and settle down."

The puppy ran inside and slid down the hall.

Angela laughed and glanced from Joy back to her pickup. "Do you feel like going somewhere or would you rather stay here?"

"Oh, I'd love to get out. With the sun shining for a change today, it would be nice to get a little fresh air. Just let me grab my coat." Joy moved back from the door and made her way to where she kept her coat and purse.

"Want me to set Bacon outside?" Angela asked as she knelt on the floor and rubbed the puppy's tummy.

"That would be great. He and Pete seem to keep each other out of trouble, at least most of the time."

Angela picked up the puppy and carried him to

the back door then set him outside. He jumped off the porch and raced around the yard, barking and yipping, trying to get Pete to play with him. Soon the donkey was chasing him like they both were dogs engaged in a grand game.

When she stepped back in the kitchen, Joy had on her coat and was tucking her house keys inside her pocket.

"Ready?" Angela asked, smiling at her friend.

"I sure am. It's so nice of you to do this, Angela. Is Nick off on another adventure today?" Joy asked as she made her way down the hall and out the door.

Angela shut it then kept step beside Joy to make sure she didn't slip on her way out to the pickup. "Nick went with two of his friends into the city. Jenny Banks took the boys. She planned to let them do some Christmas shopping, take them to see Santa one more time, if they wished, and then she said if she wasn't exhausted, she might let them go ice skating."

"Sounds like an exhausting day for her, but fun for the boys." Joy accepted Angela's help in getting up onto the passenger seat of the pickup.

Angela set Joy's crutches in the back seat then hurried around to slide behind the wheel. "Your wish is my command. Where would you like to go?"

"How about the café? Barbara makes a great cup of hot chocolate and the best chocolate chip cookies."

"That sounds great." Angela turned around and headed to the café. In a stroke of luck, she found a parking space near the door. She was just helping Joy out when Cedar Haynes hurried over with Holly Jones.

"Hi! What are you girls doing?" Holly asked as she and Cedar helped Joy out and Angela handed her the crutches.

"Nick is off with friends and the house was too quiet with him gone, so I went to visit Joy, but it's such a pretty day, we decided to come get hot chocolate and cookies." Angela smiled at Holly. The nurse fairly glowed, from the top of her shiny red curls, to the light sparkling in her gray eyes. No wonder Seth had fallen head over heels in love with her. "Did I hear congratulations are in order?"

Holly nodded and held out her hand, showing off a wide platinum band with a diamond set into the center. "Seth and I want a simple wedding at the ranch, but we're waiting until Sam can walk me down the aisle. Maybe we'll shoot for after Drew and Joy's Valentine's Day wedding."

"Sounds like a great plan to me," Angela said, giving the woman a joyful hug. "I'm so happy for you both."

The four women entered the café and took seats at a table by the front window. Barbara bustled over and took their orders then soon returned with mugs of hot chocolate and a plate full of cookies. "Enjoy, girls!" she said then disappeared in the kitchen.

"What brings you into town today?" Angela asked Holly.

"Seth needed to pick up a few supplies and asked me to come along. Sam is well enough he doesn't need someone there to help him all the time now."

"That's great news," Joy said, smiling at Holly then turning to Cedar. "What about you? What brings you into town and away from your lovely home?"

"I wanted to take a walk while the weather cooperated. Lolly tagged after me to the end of the driveway, then she went back to the pasture." Cedar grinned as she looked at Angela. "She's been fine since that episode she had the other day that forced me and Rhett to talk. If I didn't know better, I'd almost think she staged it. Then again, that silly camel spends as much time at my house as she does at Rhett's."

"Maybe it will all be one and the same soon," Holly teased, giving Cedar a nudge with her elbow as they sat together on one side of the booth.

"Perhaps Santa and Lolly can help things along," Joy said, holding up her mug in toast. "To the funny, friendly beasts of Faraday, and the humans who love them."

The women clinked their mugs together then Joy pointed out the window. "Holy hotness! Look at our very own league of extraordinary gentlemen loitering on the sidewalk."

Angela leaned around Joy and saw Drew in his postal uniform with the heavy mailbag hanging off one brawny shoulder talking to Rhett. The breeze sent the mechanic's curly hair into a tempting dance as he grinned and laughed at something Drew said. Seth stood beside him and thumped him on the shoulder as he tipped back his dark cowboy hat. Drake shook his head and scowled at his brother then motioned at something down the street beyond the ability for the women to see.

"I wonder what they're discussing?" Holly said as she took a sip of her chocolate and smiled. "Wouldn't you like to be able to crack open the window and listen?"

"I think I'd rather just imagine our heroic hunks are planning to save the world, or at least spread more Christmas cheer around town," Cedar said. "They really are such hardworking, honest, loyal, fantastic men. You pegged them right, Joy. They truly are extraordinary."

"I agree. Although I'm partial to the hunky mailman." Joy grinned. "I think we're better off not knowing what they're saying. You know how guys are. They're only a step or two removed from primitive cavedwellers sometimes. We'd probably be totally disgusted, confused, or annoyed. Let's just pretend they're discussing how they're going to treat us all like queens and spoil us rotten for Christmas."

The women laughed loudly, drawing the attention of the men. The men quickly hurried inside. Drew rushed over to Joy and kissed her cheek. "What are you doing here, baby?"

"Angela came for a visit and we decided to go on an outing. We just happened to run into Cedar and Holly."

"I thought you were at home tormenting Lolly," Rhett said, gently wrapping his hands around Cedar's neck and tipping her head back so he could kiss her full on the lips over the back of the booth.

She sighed dreamily before she grinned. "I decided to take a little walk and my feet carried me into town. I was on my way to see you when I ran into Holly coming out of Mrs. Pith's store. She said Seth was picking up supplies so we decided to come to the café to warm up for a bit."

"And here we all are," Joy said, waving a hand around the table as Drew took a drink from her mug of chocolate and snatched a cookie.

"I've got to get back to work. I'll catch you all later," Drew said, giving Joy a sweet kiss before he grabbed a second cookie and hurried outside.

"We better get going, too, Holly. Pops will be wondering what kept us this long as it is." Seth took Holly's hand as she stood and tipped his hat to the other women at the table. "We'll see everyone at the school concert, won't we?"

"Wouldn't miss it," Angela said, giving the rancher a smile. "It was great to see you, Holly. Give Ivy and Rudy some love from me."

"I'll be sure to do that," Holly said, waving as Seth guided her outside and over to his pickup.

"Come on, gorgeous," Rhett said, pulling Cedar to her feet and holding her coat while she slipped it on. "You can help me at the garage for a minute then I'll drive you home."

Angela thought they made such a striking couple. Both of them were tall. Cedar's light blond hair and sapphire blue eyes contrasted nicely to Rhett's dark curls and striking green eyes. They would certainly make beautiful babies.

Surprised by the direction of her thoughts, Angela grinned and waved as Rhett and Cedar departed.

Drake sat down in Holly's vacated seat and helped himself to a cookie. "Are you doing okay, Joy?"

"Getting better every day. The doctor has me doing therapy. I'll just be glad when I can put weight on my leg again. If I never have to see another pair of crutches after this, it will be way too soon. On the upside, though, if it wasn't for my fall, Drew might never have come to my rescue, and we wouldn't be ridiculously in love."

Angela smiled, wishing she and Drake were ridiculously in love. The odd look he gave her made her shift uncomfortably on her chair. Her phone chimed and she pulled it from her pocket. Jenny would be back with the boys in about fifteen minutes.

She sent a text letting Jenny know she'd pick Nick up at her house since she was in town anyway.

"Nick's on his way back. I better take you home, Joy. It's really been fun to visit with you today." Angela stood and handed Joy her crutches then dug in her wallet and left money on the table to join the bills those who'd already departed left to pay for the cookies and hot chocolate.

"I was about to go stir crazy, Angela. I'm so grateful you stopped by. Feel free to come anytime," Joy said as Drake held the café door open and she took careful steps outside on her crutches.

Angela inadvertently brushed against Drake as she made her way outside. The decadent masculine smell of him made her take a deep breath, until she realized what she was doing.

Annoyed with herself, with the feelings she had for him that she had no hope of controlling, she hurried to open the door to her pickup. Drake helped Joy inside then set her crutches in the back seat.

When Joy closed her door, Drake pulled Angela around to the driver's side where his brother's fiancé couldn't easily see them. Slowly, he slid one hand into Angela's hair and wrapped the other around her waist while his hot gaze tangled with hers.

Even if she'd wanted to protest, which she did not, Angela couldn't have gathered enough wits to do it as she looked into Drake's face. Fiery sparks danced in the blue depths of his eyes and a slight grin tipped the corners of his mouth up as his head lowered to hers.

She didn't know what she was expecting, but it wasn't the tender, sweet blending of their lips. That brief connection left her aching so badly for him that her whole body felt like a quivering mass. Never had she experienced such a kiss, one full of love and hope and passion.

Without a word, Drake released her then shoved his hands in his pockets. He didn't even glance back at her as he turned and strolled down the street.

Angela took several calming breaths before she could uproot her feet to carry her inside the pickup to take Joy home.

Who did Drake Miller think he was, giving her the best kiss she'd ever had then strolling off like nothing had happened?

Chapter Eleven

A loud thump outside drew Angela and Nick's gaze from their plates as they ate their dinner.

"What's that, Mom?" Nick asked as he slid out of his chair.

"I'm not sure, baby. Stay here." Angela made her way to the front of the house and flicked on the porch light. She glanced out the window and could see a green branch. "What in the world?" she muttered as she jerked open the door to find a six-foot tall fir tree standing there with a big red tag tied to the front that read, "For Nick."

Quickly maneuvering around the tree she stepped outside, but no one was there. In fact, she hadn't heard a vehicle and no taillights were visible on the lane between her house and the road. Surely someone hadn't parked at the clinic and carried the tree all the way over.

She could think of one person who would go to that much effort.

Drake.

The man was infuriating, exasperating, and completely… marvelous. Since that mind-numbing kiss he'd sprung on her, she couldn't think of anything else but how much she wanted another. How dare he kiss her like that and then walk away?

"What is it, Mom?" Nick asked as he slowly tiptoed forward.

Angela sighed and grasped the trunk of the tree, shoving it inside the house. Whoever brought it had already trimmed the bottom and fastened it in a stand. A grunt escaped her as she wrangled the tree toward the front window.

"A tree, Mommy! It's a tree!" Nick yelled, jumping up and down in excitement. "A real, live tree!"

"It sure is, baby." Angela turned the tree around so Nick could see the big tag. "It's your tree."

"Wow!" he said, sliding the tag off the branch then looking up at Angela. "Do you think Santa brought it?"

"Santa? No, he's very busy getting ready for Christmas Eve, but I bet one of his very helpful elves did." Angela went to the kitchen and returned with a pitcher of water, pouring it into the stand of the tree. The fragrance of the fir filled the house with a wonderful, nostalgic scent she loved.

"Smell that, Nick?" she said, taking a deep breath. Her son followed her example. "That smells like Christmas!"

"Christmas!" Nick echoed and gave her a big hug.

She patted his back and led him to the kitchen. "Hurry and finish your dinner then we'll decorate the tree."

Nick cleaned his plate in record time and could hardly stand still as Angela quickly did the dishes and put away the leftovers.

"Come on, Mom! Hurry!" Nick took her hand and pulled her into the living room.

Angela laughed and picked up the box containing their tree lights. After she checked to make sure they worked, Nick helped her string the lights on the tree.

"It already looks great, Mom," Nick said, bouncing on the balls of his feet as he stared at the tree. "What's next?"

"The ribbon," Angela said, taking three large spools of red and white gingham ribbon and draping it like garland around the tree branches.

"Now can we do ornaments?" Nick asked, barely about to contain his wiggles as he stood by the plastic tote holding the ornaments.

"Go for it, baby, but be careful. Some of them are breakable," Angela said, holding back a laugh as Nick took off the lid and tossed it aside then gently pulled out a glass ball that said "baby's first Christmas."

Angela sat on the couch and lifted the tattered old cardboard box that held her grandmother's Christmas treasures.

Resolved to plowing through her pain for the sake of her son, she opened the lid and closed her eyes as the scent of bayberry and sweet memories engulfed her.

Angela lifted out a shoebox full of ornaments Granny had made from old metal cookie cutters and sheet music. Granny had always been crafty that way and could make something wonderful out of seemingly nothing.

She could almost hear her granny saying, "Make do or do without, sweetheart."

For some reason, Angela thought of Drake. Since she couldn't figure out how to make do with the broken pieces of her heart, she'd learned to do without.

She took out a set of blown glass bells Papa had bought Granny for their tenth Christmas together. The glass shimmered and shined in the light from the tree and the flames of the gas fireplace she'd flicked on earlier. Gently setting them on the couch beside her, she dug back in the box and lifted out a bright pink envelope, Granny's favorite color. Angela's name was written across the front in Granny's distinctive feathery script.

Angela opened the card and gaped at the picture of an angel. Not just any angel, but one that looked exactly like her. From the dark blond hair flowing in waves around her, to the chocolate brown of the eyes, the angel bore a striking resemblance to her. A soft light seemed to glow from the angel's heart, right through the beautiful white gown she wore. Behind her, wings tipped with glitter poked out from either side of each shoulder and reflected the light.

"Oh, Granny," Angela whispered, lightly touching the front of the card before she opened it. When she did, Granny's lilac perfume floated up to her and made her eyes blur with tears. She took a moment to gather her composure. Last year, when she and Nick had gone back to Tennessee to spend Christmas with Granny, she'd known something was wrong, but Granny wouldn't tell her what. The woman seemed a little tired, a little pale, but otherwise fine. When Angela threatened to call her doctor and find out if all was well, Granny threw such a fit, Angela let it go.

Then two weeks into January, she got a call from one of Granny's neighbors, letting her know Granny was gone. Her beloved grandmother had walked out to the mailbox and died of heart failure. Granny had known for months her heart was worn out, but she didn't want Angela to worry, so she didn't say a word about it until it was too late for last goodbyes, last hugs, a last thank you for loving her when no one else did.

The anger she felt then pricked at her now, but she pushed it away. Granny had done what she thought was best, even if she deprived Angela of the privilege of caring for her during her last days. But Granny wouldn't have wanted it any other way. Angela knew that, but it didn't make it any easier.

With another cleansing breath, she focused on the words her grandmother had written in the card.

My darling Angela,

If you are reading this then know that I'm no longer in pain and your Papa and I are smiling down on you with love and pride.

You're probably still pitching a fit that I didn't tell you I was about to die when you were here for Christmas. I should have told you, honey, but I didn't want our last Christmas together to be full of tears and sadness. We both needed to make more happy memories, which is what we did (except when you got all stubborn about calling the doctor. You should know you won't win an argument with me!). I don't regret it and I'm glad we had those final days at Christmas just to laugh and enjoy one another.

Please let go of your grief and move on. If I know you, you probably even hated the thought of celebrating Christmas this year. In fact, if you are reading this note before Christmas Eve, I'll be ten kinds of surprised.

Angela smiled. "I'm days ahead of schedule, Granny."

From the day you were born, you've been a special little light from heaven that I was honored to hold not only in my arms, but also in my heart. If your mother would have allowed it, I would have raised you as my own.

So many times I wished I'd just run off with you

when you came to stay for Christmas or the summer. We could have changed our names and gone far away where no one would find us. Had I done that, you would have been spared the tragedy of marrying Allen. Not a single doubt in my mind exists that your mother pushed you into that ill-fated union. I think in some ways, she thought in her convoluted mind that by convincing you to marry him, she somehow got a second chance at life and love.

Your father, my only living child, is a drunken idiot. How he could be such a distant, foolish man is beyond my ability to understand, but he is all the same.

I'm sorry, dear one, for the misery you've suffered first from your parents then that horrid man you married. The one good thing to come from it all is Nick. That boy... oh, how he makes me smile.

Don't fret another second about him turning out like his father. He won't. Nick is just like you, full of light and love, so much love. He'll grow up to be a great man. A man who is kind and sweet, and caring.

I have no doubt Nick will turn out just fine.

You're the one I'm worried about clear down to my bones, though, honey. Between Allen and your parents, they tore you down until there was hardly anything left. You've gained some of it back over the years, but you need to learn to trust yourself, to trust your instincts, and trust your heart.

Yes, your heart.

Don't try and tell yourself you loved that wretch, Allen. I knew when I came to your wedding you didn't love him. I also knew something was wrong with him, even if I couldn't pinpoint what. I know we talked about you calling off the wedding that morning, but you were so afraid of what your mother and Allen would do, you went ahead with it. I'm sorry, honey, that I didn't drag you out of there before you committed your life to that monster.

But I digress. Here's what I know: you're smart, intelligent, independent, capable, funny, amazing, and beautiful. Any man would be fortunate to love you, and blessed to be loved by you.

Don't let the fear of the past keep you from a happy future, honey. Unless I miss my guess, you're in love with Drake Miller. Your face positively glows when you talk about him. From what you've shared, I think he loves you, too, even if you are too stubborn to admit it and too afraid to believe in it.

Let go of the doubts and worries and fears. You've always been my sweet angel, but it's time for you to open your heart to true love and spread your wings.

I love you, Angela, with all my heart and then some.

Take good care of Nick and spend your life loving and being loved by a good, honest man. Maybe once in a while think of your old Granny.

Have a wonderful Christmas, sweetness, and a happy rest of your life.

Angel kisses!
Granny

P.S. I had my friend Louella paint this card a while back. Even if you don't see it, others see that special light shining in you.

Angela couldn't contain her tears. They rolled down her cheeks in great salty drops she tried to wipe away with her sleeve.

"Mommy? What's wrong?" Nick asked, coming over and placing his little hands on her knees.

"Oh, baby, I just miss Granny so much." Angela set aside the box and card then pulled her son into her arms. She didn't want him to see her cry, didn't want him to witness her falling apart, but she couldn't stem the tide now that the dam had burst free.

"I miss her, too, Mommy, but Granny's happy and she loves us." Nick patted her cheeks and gave her a sweet smile. "It's okay, Mommy. I know Granny's just fine."

Angela drew in a shaky breath. "How do you know that?"

"Jasper and Shep told me." Nick brushed at her tears with the cuff of his sweatshirt. "Everything will be fine, Mommy. I promise. Jasper and Shep wouldn't fib."

Concerned by her son's imaginary conversations with a bird and ram, she didn't have the strength to deal with it at the moment. It was taking all her fortitude not to curl into a ball and sob until she didn't have a single tear left. How could Granny have known how she felt about Drake? How had the woman figured out Angela would back away from love, afraid she'd make another grievous mistake. If she did, it wouldn't just affect her, but Nick, too.

Granny was right, though. She'd never loved Allen. Not like a woman should love her husband. He'd been charming and flattering, but even before they wed, he'd shifted much of that attention from her to her mother. Allen had been a master manipulator and was accustomed to getting what he wanted by any means possible.

Angela was a fool for not seeing things clearly before she let her mother push her into marriage. She should have listened to Granny when she told her to walk away and not look back. Then again, if she had, she'd never have known the joy of having Nick. Her son was worth anything she had to go through to get him. Anything.

"So what's Drake worth?" Granny's voice echoed in her head.

"Everything, Granny. He's worth everything." Angela whispered, giving Nick a hug. She rose to her feet, filled with new purpose and determination. "Come on, baby, we've got a tree to decorate and plans to make."

Chapter Twelve

Drake counted to ten, hoping to gather a sense of calm in the maelstrom buzzing around him. Students raced around backstage, searching for missing costumes, giggling, and, in the case of the high school students, shamelessly flirting.

The night of the annual school Christmas program was one he generally enjoyed. Tonight, though, he felt as full of jumbled nerves as many of the students.

His first graders would perform right after the

kindergarten class sang two songs. The school had one music teacher all the grades shared, so some of the teachers, like Drake, helped where they could. He'd worked with his students for weeks to learn their songs and the accompanying motions.

Right after the program, Santa Claus would make an appearance, giving all the kids bags of treats. This year, the program signaled the last school activity until classes reconvened after the New Year.

Drake was ready for the break. His head and heart were in such a muddled mess, he needed time to sort things out.

He had no idea what had possessed him to kiss Angela on Saturday. Did he regret it? No. Not at all. What he regretted was not doing a better job of it when he had a chance.

Joy had tattled to Drew that he'd finally kissed Angela and his brother had been relentless in teasing him about not stealing the pretty vet's breath away when he had the chance.

Drew was right. He should have kissed her like there was no tomorrow. Had he done that, perhaps she would have returned his fervor. Instead, he'd given her a timid kiss and walked away like an idiot.

If he couldn't get past his feelings for her or get even the tiniest glimmer of hope she might return his feelings, he wasn't sure what he'd do.

"Need some help?" a soft hand settled on his arm while a soft voice settled in his ears. He turned and smiled at the object of his thoughts and affection.

"Hey. What are you doing back here?" he asked as Angela smiled at him. He'd been so busy with school and various obligations, he'd not had time to pursue stealing another kiss with her even if he wanted to. Which he admittedly did.

He took in the beautiful cranberry-colored dress she wore that accented her curves. Accustomed to seeing her in scrubs and cargo pants, it was easy to forget she had a killer figure. The day they'd gone skiing and she'd come out in a form-fitting knit shirt, he'd about lost his self control. Only by sheer force of will had he held onto it all day with a tenuous grasp.

"You look amazing," he said, wanting to reach out to touch the waves of her hair that slid over her shoulders and down her back.

"You look pretty good yourself," she said. Warmth shimmered in her eyes, making them look like melted chocolate.

Drake really did have a thing for all things chocolate, particularly when it came to Angela. "Do you really want to help?" He waved a hand in front of him to indicate the chaos erupting around them.

Angela nodded. "Yes. Nick is sitting with the rest of his class, ready to perform. Thanks to your diligence, they are all behaving much, much better than the kindergartners or the second graders."

He grinned. "And they've been warned Santa is watching. That helps."

A laugh spilled out of her. "It certainly does." She took a step closer to him. The temperature suddenly felt tropical as he fought to keep his hands to himself. "Did you, by chance, leave a tree at my house the other evening?"

"Me?" Drake slapped a hand to his chest in feigned innocence. "A tree?" He narrowed his gaze, pretending to consider the possibility. "What did this tree look like?"

"Green. Bushy. Fragrant. Lovely." She smiled again and squeezed his hand. "Thank you for doing that. I would have eventually got one before Christmas Eve, but I truly appreciated the help."

"If I run into the elf who delivered it for Santa, I'll let him know you liked it."

Before she could say anything, two of the other teachers came over and begged for help. Drake didn't have a chance to speak to Angela again throughout the program.

He proudly watched his students perform their lively rendition of "The Friendly Beasts" then they recited a poem about a happy snowman and the donkey that ate his nose. The class wrapped up their performance by singing a cute little song about Santa that allowed them to stomp their feet each time they sang "Ho, Ho, Ho."

Loud applause made the children smile and bow as they finished and trooped off the stage at the back of the gymnasium. Once the kids were settled in their seats, Drake returned behind the stage to help with some of the other classes.

No major calamities occurred and each grade made it through their performance. At the end, the high school students sang "Here Comes Santa Claus" while the younger students anxiously awaited the appearance of the man in red. Sleigh bells jangled and some hearty "ho, hos" rang out then Santa strode down the aisle and to a chair set at the base of the stage for him to sit in while he passed out treats.

Drake watched as Angela recorded Nick going up to Santa and whispering something to him before he took a bag. The little boy skipped back to where Angela sat with Drake's family and friends. Her friends. They'd be her family, too, if she'd just give them and him a chance.

Heart sore and tired, Drake missed it when Santa called his name.

The health teacher gave him a nudge. "Go on, Drake. Santa's got something for you."

"Huh?" Drake hurried down the stage steps and over to Santa. To give the crowd some laughs, he sat down on Santa's lap and accepted the bag the man held out to him.

"For a tall, lean guy, you're heavier than you look, man," Santa groused.

"Just giving them a good show, Santa," Drake grinned as he stood and took the bright red bag, heading toward the back of the stage. Then the crowd started chanting "open it, open it, open it!"

Drake shrugged and started to untie the ribbon holding the bag shut then noticed a tag.

Drake -
Your mom said she'd pass this torch to me, but only if I promise to buy them for you every year until we're old and gray. Are you game? If so, nod yes.
XOXO
Your Christmas Angel

A quick glance melded his gaze to Angela's. Eager and excited, he nodded his head then tore the tissue paper out of the bag and grinned as he stared down at the abominable snowman's face.

Embarrassing as it was, he pulled the underwear from the bag and held them up for the crowd to see. He turned around and held them at his waist and waggled his rear back and forth a few times, drawing hoots and cheers from the crowd before everyone got up to go to the cafeteria for refreshments.

Angela said something to Nick and sent him off with Drake's parents to get punch and cookies. She turned back to where Drake stood near Santa's now empty chair. He grinned and she smiled then raced toward him.

He dropped the bag and underwear and swept her into his arms.

"Really, Angel? You'll really, really be mine?" he asked, swinging her around then stopping long enough to set her down so he could bracket her face with hands and look into her eyes.

The love and hope that shone there filled his heart to overflowing. She was his! Angela was no longer holding herself back, hiding behind walls, or shutting him out. Her heart was wide open, just waiting for him to walk inside.

"I love you, Drake. I think I have since the day I ran into you with my cart."

His thumb traced the line of her jaw. "I know I've loved you since then. This isn't the time or place to ask, Angel, but will you marry me? Will you buy me ridiculous underwear every Christmas and make me slow cooker cake, and fill my world with your love?"

"Yes, Drake! Yes, yes, yes!" Angela pulled his head down and kissed him.

It took only a second for Drake to take charge, letting the love he'd carried in his heart for this woman the last three years pour into that one passionate, perfect kiss.

"I love you so much, Drake," Angela said when they stopped to catch their breath. "Thank you for loving me even when I was afraid to follow my heart."

"I told you before, Angel, I'm not going anywhere. I'll always be here for you. Nick, too."

Angela grinned and rested her head against his chest. Drake wrapped her in his arms, relishing the feel of holding her close to his heart. He'd waited so long and now his dreams were finally coming true. "I figured out what Nick wants for Christmas."

"You did? What is it? A bike? A rocket? A tool set so he can play with Rhett in the garage?" Drake asked.

Angela laughed. "No, although the tool set isn't a bad idea, but Rhett might not think so. What Nick really wants for Christmas is a dad. Thanks to your brother, I got the letter Nick mailed to Santa. That's all he wanted this year was a dad, and not just any dad. In his letter, he specifically asked for his teacher, Mr. Miller, to be his dad. He mentioned something about Jasper told him it could happen."

"Really? He wants me for his dad?" Drake choked on the last word. He loved Nick like a son, but he'd barely dared to dream he might one day be a father to him. "I'll do my best to make a good dad to him, and husband to you."

Angela touched a finger to the dimple in his chin and grinned. "You'll be a fabulous dad and an amazing husband, Drake. I don't have a single doubt in my mind. Granny left me a note that put things in perspective."

"Granny?" Drake asked, then a look of panic settled on his face. "Oh, my gosh! With the concert and program tonight, I forgot about Jasper. We better go check on him."

He and Angela hurried back to his classroom. Drake flicked on the light and the bird started cooing, hopping from one perch to another in his cage.

"I think he wants out," Angela said, opening the door to his cage and lifting Jasper out. He squirmed and fussed, so she set him down on the table. The bird looked at her and cooed, then tipped his head toward Drake and cooed more.

"We should take him home for the break," she said. "If you carry his cage out to my pickup, I'll take him home with me."

"Sure. When we're ready to leave, we can…" Drake grabbed for the bird when he flapped his wings and flew out of the room.

He and Angela raced after Jasper into the hallway. One of the teachers just happened to open the main door outside at that moment and the bird made a beeline for it.

"Jasper! No! Wait," Angela called.

Drake took her hand in his as they ran to the door. Together, they watched the dove take flight into the midnight velvet sky. The school lights made his wings look almost translucent as he rose upward and disappeared. A single white feather drifted down to them.

Angela caught it and gave Drake an odd look.

Nick ran outside and took the feather in his hand. "It's okay, Mom. Jasper told me goodbye earlier. He said he couldn't stay for Christmas but Granny says to tell you to buy Rudolph next year."

"Rudolph?" Drake asked, confused. He picked up Nick and settled his other arm around Angela's shoulders. Together, they headed toward the school's front door as snow began to fall.

"Underwear," Angela said, staring at Nick in stunned surprise. "I couldn't decide between the abominable snowman or Rudolph underwear."

Nick just giggled then gave Drake a tight hug. "When can I start calling you Dad, Mr. Miller?" he asked.

"Just as soon as your mom decides on a wedding date."

Nick beamed. "I can't wait! This is the best Christmas ever! Santa already brought my Christmas present and it's not even Christmas Eve yet!"

Drake hugged him back then set him down. "Thank you, Nick, for wanting me to be your dad. I promise to give it my best."

The little boy grinned. "I know you will. Jasper told me you're the daddy I was always meant to have. I'm gonna go tell Uncle Drew and Aunt Joy. They said I could call them that when Mom gave you the underwear."

Nick ran off but turned back when Drake pulled Angela to him once more. "Give him a good kiss, Mommy. I think dads like that sort of thing."

Drake chuckled as Nick scurried back inside. He rested his forehead against Angela's and kissed her nose. "You know, dads do like that sort of thing. I think I'll need lots of practice, though." Drake kissed her cheek. "I'll marry you tomorrow, if that's what you want, Angel, or a year from now, just as long as you'll eventually be mine."

"Oh, I think a year is far, far too long for Nick to wait to get his Christmas wish." Angela wrapped her arms around his neck. "Maybe we can start off the new year as a brand new family."

"I can't think of anything I'd like better." Drake kissed her again, filled with love and wonder that this woman, this magnificent woman, truly loved him. "I love you, my sweet Christmas Angel."

"And I love you, Drake." She pulled back from him and tossed him a saucy grin. "Even if you have terrible taste in underwear." She squealed and raced ahead of him out of the snow and into the warmth of a future full of promise and hope.

Epilogue

Christmas Eve

"It's about time you got here," Lolly said, smiling at Jasper as the dove landed on a brace holding up the stable for the nativity play.

"You do know I hate the cold and have spent the last month sitting in Drake's toasty classroom getting overfed and under-exercised, don't you?" Jasper flapped a wing at her. "I think my feet are frozen."

"We all know you hate the cold, Jasper, but welcome to winter in the mountains." Lolly grinned at him. "And you did a great job with your part in helping our stubborn, clueless humans finally find true love."

"I thought I'd actually given myself brain damage when I flew into Drake's classroom window, but turns out I was fine and it sure helped get those two together," Jasper cooed.

"Jasper and I really worked hard to get Drake and Angela to admit their love. She is one independent thinker, but they are planning a New Year's Eve wedding. Nick told me Angela wants to have it up at the lodge," Shep said, rubbing his curly horn on the makeshift fence encircling them on the town square.

"Knock that off, ram head. If you tip over the fence, it'll distract the guys and they need to stay focused on the girls," Ivy said as she glared at Shep then gave her young son a motherly scowl. "Rudy, get back over here. I don't want you getting too close to all the grubby little hands reaching through the fence tonight. Who knows that you might catch from them."

"Yes, mama," Rudy said. The calf trotted back and cuddled against her side.

"He's just precious, Ivy," Lolly said, smiling at the cow. "And it worked out great that Holly helped Seth take care of him."

"It did, although I didn't intend for Rudy to get stuck out in the cold and get sick. But Holly was a huge help. Even Seth noticed it." Ivy blew out a puff of air. "I'm so excited they're getting married as soon as Sam is back on his feet."

The animals moved aside as a horse trailer

backed up to the pen and watched as Rhett and Drew opened the back and led out a donkey wearing a Santa hat with a brown puppy trailing his every step.

"Hey, Pete! Welcome to the party. I see you brought your sidekick along," Lolly said, moving over to the donkey as Rhett closed the gate behind him. "For those who haven't yet met the newest members of the Friendly Beasts of Faraday, this is Pete and his little buddy, Bacon. We're excited to have you both join us. I hope you'll plan on it every year."

Pete bobbed his head. "As long as I can stay in here with you all and not have to give rides or anything, I'll pencil it in." The donkey watched as Drew carried Joy over to a bench. "I thought we'd never get those two together. Bacon, young as he is, was a big help."

"It was brilliant, busting out of your yard and hustling over to mine." Lolly moved alongside Pete then dropped her head to give Bacon a welcoming grin. She sighed happily as Drew bent down and kissed Joy's cheek. "By the time they found you, a blind bat could have seen the sparks flying between the two of them. When is the wedding?"

"Valentine's Day. I heard Joy saying something about hearts and romance. I've tried to warn Drew, but he gives me the weirdest looks when I talk to him," Pete said, shaking snow off his mane. He tossed Bacon a warning look to stay put when the puppy started to wander off. The little canine plopped his fuzzy rump in the snow next to the donkey. "Did you hear about Joy's care packages?"

"Care packages?" Shep asked.

"She made up baskets full of goodies to take to all the old people in our neighborhood and she made gifts for everyone who helped her while she's been stuck on the crutches unable to get around." Pete gave his owner an admiring glance. "She continues to live up to her name, bringing joy to those around her."

"She certainly brought it to Drew, if the smile on his face is any indication," Ivy observed. "A year ago, I was convinced these guys were completely hopeless."

Lolly chuckled. "Not completely hopeless. Just look at them. Even my Rhett found love this holiday season. I adore Cedar. She gives the best neck scratches ever. I think she's going to make him happier than he ever dreamed possible."

"Only if he gets around to proposing." Ivy tipped her head in the direction of where their humans were gathered. Rhett and Cedar stood with her sister, Juniper, as well as Seth, Holly, Drake and Drew. Angela and Nick sat next to Joy and Sam on the bench in front of them.

Lolly turned and glared at the cow. "I know for a fact he's got a ring in his pocket and plans to pop the question tonight, when the time is just right."

"Oh! A Christmas Eve proposal. That's splendid," Jasper cooed, then glanced down at Pete. "What's with the hat, dude?"

"It keeps my head warm and Joy thinks it cute." Pete dropped his head down as a little girl stuck her hand through the fence, trying to reach him. He let the toddler brush the soft fur along his jaw and batted his eyes at her.

"Flirt," Ivy teased.

"She's kind of cute, for one of those little rugrats." Pete moved back as the humans in the nativity play approached in their costumes.

"Just wait until next year. Maybe our people will have babies of their own. I sure hope Rhett and Cedar have one. I bet it would be adorable." Lolly tipped her head toward the audience. "Here come the wise men. If they are wise, they won't try riding me again this year."

Shep snorted. "I'd like to see them try."

Lolly tossed him a crooked smile then looked around her group of friends. "Merry Christmas, gang. I'd say our plans worked out perfectly. May this be the beginning of another blessed year and a lifetime of happiness for our humans."

Chocolate Lava Cake

The gooey, decadent deliciousness of chocolate lava cake gets even better when you can make it in a slow cooker, especially when it makes its own topping while it cooks! Enjoy this easy recipe!

Cake:
1 chocolate cake mix
3 eggs
1 ¼ cups milk
½ cup vegetable oil
Topping:
1 large box instant chocolate pudding mix
2 cups milk
12 ounce bag chocolate chips

With an electric mixer, combine cake mix, oil, eggs and 1 ¼ cups milk on medium speed until batter is smooth.

Spray a slow cooker with non-stick spray. Pour the mixture into the slow cooker.

Beat together the remaining milk with pudding mix and pour over the top. Do not stir. Sprinkle chocolate chips over the top. Again, do not stir.

Cover and cook on high for 2 ½ hours. The cake is done when the outsides and top are sponge-like and the middle is gooey. Serve with vanilla ice cream. Makes approximately 10 servings.

Note: Cook times can vary depending on the size and shape of your slow cooker. If yours is taller and not wide, it may take longer. Keep an eye on the cake when to be sure it doesn't burn.

Author's Note

It started with a camel.

A few years ago, Captain Cavedweller and I were at a community event and there, in all his fuzzy, giant glory, was a big camel, just eating up the attention.

The overactive part of my imagination that never shuts off began to mull over the idea of a camel bringing a couple together. How could that happen? What would it look like?

What if there wasn't just a camel, but an entire cast of crazy, funny animals doing their best to play matchmakers?

Then the words from a Christmas song drifted through my head and I knew exactly what I wanted to do.

You see, that Christmas song is called "The Friendly Beasts." It's about the gifts animals present to Jesus in the manger. The origins of the song go all the way back to 12th century France, but the modern English words were penned in the 1920s.

Artists from Burl Ives to the Mormon Tabernacle Choir have performed the song, but my favorite version is from Garth Brooks on his *Beyond the Season* Christmas album. And I highly recommend looking up the lyrics, too, because they're not only fun, but will also add an element of understanding as to why I chose such specific animals for these four stories.

Once I'd decided the series would be about a bunch of loveable, wacky animals meddling in the lives of four unsuspecting couples, I had to figure out the rest of the details.

I wanted the story's setting to be in Oregon. It had to be somewhere with snow for the story to work, but also close to a bigger city or town. That's when I decided to create the fictional town of Faraday on the way up the mountain to Mount Hood.

The details about the lodge are from the existing Timberline Lodge located there.

I had the animals, the idea, and the setting.

All I needed then were the characters. I started thinking about who would own each of these unique pets. That spurred the idea of four friends who'd known each other from childhood.

Of course, the camel had to be the lead story. But who would own a camel? And not just any camel, but a Bactrian camel. The answer to that came in the idea of an eccentric uncle to the hero of the first story. It wouldn't seem strange for a man who collects any number of odd things to add a camel to the mix.

I liked the idea of a mechanic who wanted to get away from the small town but found himself back there (and grudgingly glad to be) when his uncle needed him. Enter Rhett — our tousle-haired mechanic with a bad boy reputation.

How perfect for his love interest to be an uptight career-focused woman recovering from a breakdown.

I kept picturing Cedar's first meeting with Lolly in my head... that moment when Cedar is trying so hard to just find her "happy place" and be filled with peace. Then she opens her eyes to find a camel staring at her through the patio door and freaks out. I could imagine her reaction, how upset she'd be with her neighbor, and Rhett pretending he didn't live across the pasture from her upon discovering she was the woman who'd called a dozen times to complain about Lolly.

How long could he keep up the ruse? What would happen when she discovered he owned the camel? Entertaining stuff, right?

I will admit, I had the most fun writing the second book in the story because the hero of Tidings of Joy is inspired by someone very near and dear to my heart (and if you are guessing, yes, that's right… Captain Cavedweller). CC has carried mail for most of the time we've been married and he's had so many adventures in that job. In fact, that's his uniform coat you see on the cover of *Tidings of Joy*.

So if I seem a little biased toward Drew Miller's character, it's only because he is based on my beloved CC. And some of those crazy experiences Drew had were actual things that have happened to CC on his mail routes (like the dead snake in the mailbox and the lion, only the lion that terrorized CC was a taxidermied lion, not a dog dressed up like one). I'll let you guess about the stapled pants incident, but even my imagination couldn't have conjured something that hilarious!

Oh, and the snack mix Drew loves is from snack mix CC used to get every year on his route. I've tried to duplicate the recipe and have not yet mastered it. Someday!

I also have to share this story: when I was in high school, one of the groups I belonged to decided to do a community service day where we went around and did helpful things in our little hometown. At one house, there was a sweet, tiny old woman who was so excited we were there. She brought out a whole pie and gave us slices, right into our hands. No napkins. Not even a paper towel. I took a bite to be polite and reacted about like Drew did. And it was mincemeat pie. I managed to choke down the bite I'd taken and hide the rest in the trunk of my friend's car until I could throw it away. That was my one and only experience with mincemeat pie!

Knowing how shy and introverted Drew's character was going to be, I wanted him to fall in love with a girl who could draw him out of his shell. Joy was perfect for that. I just loved her character and how full of joy she was even with her injury. And Joy's Christmas birthday is a nod to my dad who was born on Christmas Day.

It didn't hurt that she was the owner of Pete and Bacon either. I giggled every time I typed Bacon's name. Don't ask me how I came up with that. I was sitting at my computer one day trying to decide what names to give all the animals and "Bacon" just kept popping up in there. (Maybe it was caused by a BLT craving.) Anyway, I adore Bacon's little character and the way he interacts with Pete the donkey. Seriously, I want my own Pete and Bacon now (and I love, love the way they look on the cover of Tidings of Joy!)

Since two schemers are better than one, it

stood to reason that with Pete and Bacon on the job, it wouldn't take long for Drew and Joy to fall in love.

If you've read many of my books, you know I thoroughly enjoy writing about cowboys. I had to include one in this series, so that's where Seth comes in. He and Rhett make rather unlikely best friends, but their relationship works because the things that bind them run deep below the surface and wind around the heart.

I liked that they were there for each other and helped one another when they needed a hand.

An older, wiser cowboy in the form of Seth's grandpa played a vital role in this story. After all, without Sam's injury, Holly would never have had a reason to come to the ranch, even if Seth had already met her (and decided he didn't like her!).

Seth, who's roots run about as deep as they can go on the ranch, falling for a woman without any ties to bind her seemed like a great combination. They give "opposites attract" a whole new definition, but at the end of the day, they have far more in common than first meets the eye.

In addition to getting a cowboy included in the series by working in a ranch as one of the settings, it provided the perfect means to work in a cow, "all white and red." That's why Ivy and baby Rudy are part of the story.

If you've ever had a sick calf you had to drench while trying to keep the mama at bay, you have my sympathies. From experience on our family farm, I know that is not an endeavor for the faint-hearted. And writing that scene into the story seemed like a good way to initiate Holly into rural life.

Don't ask me why I gave Holly such a whackadoodle name. It just came to me and insisted on being included. I could envision her mother as a hippie who idolized Florence Nightingale, yet had a strange sense of humor, too.

And that scene where Sam puts bacon on Holly's plate (maybe I really was hungry for bacon while I was writing these stories!)... I just thought it would be amusing for these two beef-raising, meat-eating ranchers to try and persuade Holly to give up her vegetarian ways.

I know I had both Rhett and Seth take their girls into the woods to get Christmas trees. I included that not just because it provided a wonderful opportunity for romance, but also because my family had a tradition of going every year to the woods. It was about an hour and a half drive from our house up to the woods. We'd often make a day of it, with my dad and brothers hauling along snowmobiles. Sometimes they'd take one of the farm trucks and cut a load of wood while we were there, too. It was such a not-to-be-missed tradition, I even went one year with a broken foot in a cast. When the doctor cut off the cast a few weeks later, pine needles fell out. Gosh, I wonder where they all came from?

With all those animals running around in Faraday, I decided we needed a youngster, too. Enter Nick, the sweet little boy of the town's veterinarian. And since the other three stories involved fairly sudden romances, I thought it would be nice for this last story if the couple had secretly been in love with each other for a while.

Angela's been hurt so badly in the past, she can't begin to the think of the future. And Drake, poor Drake, can hardly think straight for loving her so much. But he's terrified of losing her friendship if he tells her the truth.

The foundation of my education took place in a small school, even smaller than the Faraday School in the story. And I absolutely adored my first-grade teacher. She was the best! And she had a treasure chest filled with all kinds of wonderful goodies that we could choose from when we excelled at something. I remember how much fun it was to walk up to her desk and pick something from it.

Another tidbit from my school days were the school cooks mentioned in this story. We had two amazing cooks who prepared delicious meals. Not only that, but they were just full of fun and took such good care of us all.

The thingamajig toy that Nick plays with is from one my grandpa made and would let me play with when I stayed at their house.

That nostalgic feeling that swept over Angela when she opened her Granny's box and the scent wafted around her? I know it well.

Every year when my mom would open a certain holiday box, the scent of bayberries and sweet memories would float out of it, embracing me with this wonderful feeling of home and Christmas and family. I know just how Angela felt when she opened her Granny's special box.

I have to mention Shep (the sheep with the curly horn) and Jasper (the dove in the rafters high).

Aren't they a fun matchmaking duo? I took great delight in imaging the conversations taking place between Jasper and Shep - and then the things the two of them whispered to Nick.

Oh, and if you didn't read the recipes at the end of each story, check them out. If you put them all together, you have an appetizer, salad, main dish, and dessert!

I extend a special note of gratitude to my editors and proofreaders. Thank you Shauna, Katrina, Leo, Cindy, Sonya, and Becky. And thanks to Jessica and Melanie for your excellent help with the book blurbs.

Without the incredible talent of Rob Foote, illustrator extraordinaire, the covers for these books, along with the amazing art piece of all the animals together would not exist. I first worked with Rob when he agreed to illustrate my children's book, *Steve the Mule*. Rob was so wonderful to work with, he immediately came to mind when I thought about covers for these four stories.

He took my crazy ideas and turned them into beautiful pieces of art that made me cry with joy when I first saw them. Thank you, Rob, for being willing to work with me again. You are fantastic and so appreciated!

Thank you, faithful readers, for coming on an adventure to the fictional town of Faraday where a fun-loving camel and her cohorts made Christmas merry and bright.

I hope this holiday season brings you and yours a bounty of joy and hope, laughter and love.

Merry Christmas from our home to yours!

Thank you for reading *Wings of An Angel*. I'd be so grateful if you'd share a <u>review</u> so other readers might discover this heartwarming holiday series. Even a line or two is appreciated more than you can know.

Read the rest of the books in the
<u>Friendly Beasts of Faraday</u> series!
Scent of Cedar
Tidings of Joy
Boughs of Holly
Wings of An Angel

Also, if you haven't yet signed up for my newsletter, won't you consider subscribing? I send it out a few times a month, when I have new releases, sales, or news of freebies to share. Each month, you can enter a contest, get a new recipe to try, and discover news about upcoming events. When you sign up, you'll receive a free short and sweet historical romance. Don't wait. Sign up today!

And if newsletters aren't your thing, please follow me on BookBub. You'll receive notifications on pre-orders, new releases, and sale books!

If you enjoyed meeting the quirky, loveable characters in the **Friendly Beasts of Faraday** series don't miss out on the Rodeo Romance series!

Rodeo Romance Series
Hunky rodeo cowboys tangle with independent sassy women who can't help but love them.

The Christmas Cowboy (Book 1) — Among the top saddle bronc riders in the rodeo circuit, easy-going Tate Morgan can master the toughest horse out there, but trying to handle beautiful Kenzie Beckett is a completely different story.

Wrestlin' Christmas (Book 2) — Sidelined with a major injury, steer wrestler Cort McGraw struggles to come to terms with the end of his career. Shanghaied by his sister and best friend, he finds himself on a run-down ranch with a worrisome, albeit gorgeous widow, and her silent, solemn son.

Capturing Christmas (Book 3) — Life is hectic on a good day for rodeo stock contractor Kash Kressley. Between dodging flying hooves and babying cranky bulls, he barely has time to sleep. The last thing Kash needs is the entanglement of a sweet romance, especially with a woman as full of fire and sass as Celia McGraw.

Barreling Through Christmas (Book 4) — Cooper James might be a lot of things, but beefcake model wasn't something he intended to add to his resume.

Chasing Christmas (Book 5) — Tired of his cousin's publicity stunts on his behalf, bull rider Chase Jarrett has no idea how he ended up with an accidental bride!

Racing Christmas (Book 6) — Brylee Barton is racing to save her family's ranch. Shaun Price is struggling to win her heart. . . again.

The combination of Christmas and hunky cowboy

May prove to be more than she can resist. . .

<u>*The Christmas Cowboy*</u> *(Rodeo Romance Book 1)* — Tate Morgan is as tough as they come. He can handle the wildest bronc on the rodeo circuit, but he loses the ability to think straight around the beautiful woman he keeps running into at the airport. Completely captivated by the uptight executive who makes it clear she detests cowboys, Tate will have to work a little holiday magic if he wants to win her heart.

Married to her job as a corporate trainer for a successful direct sales company, Kenzie Beckett doesn't have time for a man. Besides, after being burned twice by two-timing losers, she refuses to allow a third opportunity to exist. Unfortunately, no one told that to the handsome rodeo cowboy who catches her eye at the airport. He'll need more than a pair of fine-fitting jeans, dusty boots, and dimpled smile to break past her resistance and bring her a heaping helping of holiday cheer.

Full of laughter and tender romance, *The Christmas Cowboy* takes readers on a sweet Christmas adventure to a happily ever after.

Turn the page for an excerpt...

The Christmas Cowboy

"This seat taken?"

Startled by the deep voice speaking close to her ear, Kenzie Beckett glanced up into eyes the color of sapphires and lost the ability to speak.

Shaking her head, she moved her oversized shoulder bag from the chair in question to a space near her feet. The intent gaze of the man made her sit up straight in the chair and fight the urge to lick her suddenly dry lips. She'd noticed the handsome cowboy at the airport many times, but never had the opportunity to be this close to him.

He smelled every bit as good as he looked.

"Mind if I sit down?" he asked, pointing to the empty chair beside her.

Nervous, but with no reason to refuse, she again shook her head. Slowly inhaling a deep breath, she smiled and stuck out her hand as the cowboy folded himself into the seat. He filled the space next to her with an appealing scent that made her think of leather, spice, and rugged masculinity.

"I'm Kenzie."

Pleased when he took her hand and gave it a firm, yet gentle shake, the contact created an unsettling storm of electrical currents to rush up her arm.

"Tate." A white-toothed grin displayed two dimples through the scruffy stubble on his face. "Tate Morgan."

"It's nice to meet you, Mr. Morgan." Tongue-tied and awestruck, Kenzie couldn't believe she sat next to Tate Morgan, rodeo star.

Although ranching and rodeos were no longer part of her life, she kept up with some of the details. The good-looking cowboy sitting next to her was one of the top saddle bronc riders in the world. She knew he was from Washington State, but never connected him to the Tri-Cities area where she lived. She absently wondered if he was from Kennewick, Richland, or Pasco.

He must frequent the Pasco airport as often as she did with his rodeo travels. That was probably why she'd seen him there before and why he was waiting in the seat next to her to board the flight to Denver.

"Where are you traveling today?"

"Tennessee," Tate replied, grateful he arrived late at the airport. The only seat left in the waiting area was the one next to the dark-haired beauty who caught his eye the last few times he flew out of town. "Call me Tate. All my friends do and I certainly hope we'll be friends."

Kenzie narrowed her gaze. She should have known he'd start flirting within seconds of sitting down. Apparently, a pair of boots, a Stetson, and perfect-fitting Wranglers gave a man free license to flirt with any female crossing his path.

"I don't make it a habit of becoming friends with people I randomly meet at the airport." She tore her gaze away from Tate's gorgeous blue eyes. Swiftly closing the fashion magazine she'd been mindlessly reading before he startled her, she stuffed it into her bag and checked her watch again.

"Really?" Tate pushed the brim of his Stetson up with an index finger and revealed a hint of light brown hair. "I figure once names are exchanged and handshakes are given, you're a friend until proven otherwise."

Heat filled her cheeks at his words. Despite his friendly tone and broad smile, she recognized a rebuke when she heard one.

What was it about this man that threw her off her game?

As a corporate trainer for one of the most successful direct sales companies in the country, she could get a room filled with consultants on their feet and enthusiastically following her direction with no problem. She could take on the corporate team, pitch ideas, and win them over to her way of thinking with hardly a blink.

But put her next to a cowboy, especially one as attractive as Tate, and she lost the ability to function with any degree of logic or wisdom.

A voice over the loudspeaker interrupted her thoughts, announcing another fifteen-minute delay for the Denver flight.

Kenzie released a pent-up sigh, opened a zippered pocket on her bag, and pulled out her phone. She sent a text message to the organizer of the regional meeting in Denver she planned to lead later that morning, informing the woman she would probably be late.

Normally, Kenzie liked to arrive the day before an event so she didn't run the risk of being late. It also gave her time to prepare to give her best to the consultants.

The trainer originally lined up to lead the meeting had an emergency and asked Kenzie to cover for him, so she'd only found out she needed to be in Denver the previous evening.

"Is everything okay?" Tate drummed his fingers on the arm of the seat. In spite of his calm facade, he had a tight connecting flight schedule and if they didn't get moving, he was going to miss his plane.

"It will be if we can board and be on our way soon," Kenzie said, tugging on the navy skirt of her business suit. The airport was warm and stuffy, crowded as it was with people waiting for flights, even though it was early May and the temperature outside was pleasant. "I'm leading a meeting in Denver and unless we make up some time in the air, a few hundred consultants will be left waiting for me to get there. I don't like to keep people waiting."

"That's good to know." He grinned again. "What is it you do?"

Kenzie glanced over to see if he was genuinely interested or just killing time. At the inquisitive look in his eyes, she relaxed a little.

"I'm a corporate trainer with Dew." Kenzie took a business card from her bag and handed it to him. "We're a skin care company that's been around since the 1940s."

Tate accepted the card from Kenzie and stared at the logo of a pale blue dewdrop with the word

"Dew" embossed in gold across the center.

"Dew?" He thought it was an odd name for a company. "Where's the name come from?"

Kenzie smiled and Tate felt drawn to the light shining in her beautiful brown eyes. They reminded him of the molasses his dad was so fond of eating - dark, rich, and sweet.

"All women want a soft, dewy complexion." She bit her tongue to keep from launching into her usual spiel about the company and their superior products.

"If they hired you to be a walking billboard, you do a great job," Tate said, causing Kenzie to blush again. "So your company is all about stuff women use to preserve their youthful appearance?"

"Basically."

Convinced the outrageously handsome cowboy next to her would not understand the importance of moisturizers, lotions, and exfoliators to the health of aging skin, she nodded her head.

Tate shot her a wicked grin. "So your people go door-to-door peddling goo?"

"No, they don't go door-to-door or peddle goo." Kenzie couldn't stop the smile lifting the corners of her mouth as she removed a catalog from her bag and handed it to Tate.

He browsed through the glossy pages, noticing the company offered more than just lotions and potions. Dew sold a collection for men, spa items, and gift options in what appeared to be a well-thought-out product line.

"How does it work? How do your... what did you call them? Consultants?" At her nod he continued. "How do they get catalogs into the hands of potential customers?" Unfamiliar with the concept of direct sales, if Tate found something he didn't know, he quickly set out to learn all he could on the topic.

"Home parties. People invite friends into their homes and host parties. Consultants give a brief presentation and take orders. The party host receives freebies and discounted product for her trouble and people get together for a fun hour or two while shopping in the comfort of someone's home," Kenzie explained, warming to the subject.

She put herself through college doing direct sales. Her passion for the industry, Dew in particular, was why she was a well-respected corporate trainer at the age of twenty-seven.

"If I invite a bunch of buddies to my house, set out some snacks and have one of your consultants come show us your stuff, you'd give me freebies?" Tate asked, only halfway joking. If he could somehow coerce Kenzie into being the consultant, he'd host a party every month just to be able to see her.

"In theory, that's how it works." She laughed as a visual popped into her head of Tate and his friends sitting around with facials dripping off their stubbly chins. "Of course, the freebies depend on your total orders for the party."

Before Tate could ask more questions, the call to board rang through the airport. Under the assumption it would take a while, Kenzie began to gather up her belongings to make a final trip to the restroom.

Tate put a hand on her arm, drawing her attention. "You can leave your stuff here. I'll keep an eye on it," he said, nodding his head toward the restroom door.

"Well, I…" Kenzie said, surprised by his offer. She didn't know the man and shouldn't trust him, even if he did seem nice.

"I promise not to run off with your stuff or touch anything." Tate held his hand up as if he made a pledge. "Scout's honor. Besides, I'd look ridiculous toting that bright pink bag. It clashes with my shirt."

She'd tried not to notice how well his burgundy shirt fit across his broad shoulders and chest.

"Thank you," she said, getting to her feet. "I'll be right back."

"No need to hurry." Tate glanced at the long line of people waiting to board.

When she returned a few minutes later, Tate stood at the back of the line, both his bag and hers over his shoulder, her suit jacket draped over his arm.

"I thought I better get in line since it's finally starting to move." He handed Kenzie her jacket.

"Thank you." She took her bag from him and slid the strap over her shoulder. Hurriedly digging in a side pocket, she pulled out her boarding pass and checked to make sure everything was just as she left it. Tate seemed like a good guy, but trusting handsome cowboys had gotten her into trouble before.

"What have you got in that thing? Rocks?" Tate teased as they stepped closer to the door.

"No, bricks." Kenzie grinned over her shoulder at him as she handed her pass to the ticket agent.

Tate felt an unfamiliar twinge in the region of his heart as Kenzie took her boarding pass and walked out the door. Regardless of his extensive experience with the opposite sex, he'd never had anyone affect him like the beautiful brunette.

As he gave her a quick once-over, he admired the dark hair piled on her head, her long legs, and trim figure. Her stature intrigued him. He generally preferred smaller women, but in her heels, Kenzie nearly met his six-foot one-inch height.

A hint of something soft and floral tickled his nose while they walked onto the plane and waited to go down the aisle. He leaned closer and breathed in her scent, deciding he'd never smelled anything quite so inviting and feminine.

Out of habit, he tugged his hat more firmly on his head and studied the harried faces on the crowded plane. He hoped the flight would go quickly. It was vital he catch the connection to Nashville where he'd meet a friend to hitch a ride to his next rodeo.

He swallowed back a grin when he located his seat and Kenzie sat across the aisle from him. Suddenly, his day looked brighter. The connecting flight concerns shuffled to the back of his mind.

Instead of worrying, he had a few hours of uninterrupted time to get to know his lovely traveling companion.

After settling in to his assigned space, Tate noticed Kenzie leaning back in her seat, eyes closed, hands gripping the armrest with white knuckles.

He reached across the aisle and placed his hand on hers, watching her eyes pop open.

"We won't crash, you know." He attempted to coax her smile out of hiding.

"I know. I just hate takeoffs. I'm fine once we get in the air." Kenzie offered Tate a tense glance. "It's that awful feeling when your stomach is weightless that gets me every time."

"That's one of the best parts of flying." He waggled an eyebrow her direction.

"It's not surprising a daredevil like you would think so." She squeezed her eyes shut when the plane roared down the runway and lifted into the air. As it gained altitude, she let out the breath she'd held and relaxed.

"How do you know what I do for a living?" Certain they hadn't gotten around to discussing why he was going to Tennessee or his career, his brow wrinkled in question as he looked at her.

"I assumed you're a daredevil by that gleam in your eye and the look on your face that says you love adventure." Kenzie wasn't willing to acknowledge she recognized Tate's name and knew exactly what he did for a living. She refused to admit to anyone, least of all the handsome cowboy beside her, she had even a passing interest in anything to do with the pro rodeo circuit. That was classified information she'd take to her grave. "You appear to be someone who lives life on the edge."

"I guess some people think I do. I ride saddle broncs as a profession. Well, at least I do when I'm not busy ranching." Tate chuckled and shook his head derisively. "What I really should say is when I'm not gone to a rodeo, I stay busy on our family ranch."

"Is that why you're traveling to Tennessee?" Kenzie asked, trying to think what rodeo he'd entered. It had been a long time since she'd kept close tabs on the rodeo circuit.

"Yep. I'm meeting a friend in Nashville and then we're off to the rodeo. We're both competing tomorrow." He removed his hat and placed it on his lap.

Kenzie admired his strong hands as he ran tanned fingers through his thick hair to loosen the band pressed into it from his hat. She wouldn't allow herself to think of that head of light brown hair. Cut short, it was just long enough to have some finger-tempting waves, absolutely meant to torment women.

"Does your friend also ride saddle broncs?" Unsuccessfully, Kenzie tried to keep her gaze from entangling with his.

From experience gained in what seemed like a lifetime ago, she knew saddle bronc riders were artists, of a sort, as well as spectacular athletes. While bull riding and bareback riding were wilder, saddle bronc riding demanded style, grace, and precision.

"Nah, he's a steer wrestler," Tate said, grateful Cort McGraw agreed to swing by the airport and pick him up on his way through Nashville.

Thoughtfully observing him, Kenzie pulled a water bottle from her bag and took a drink. Once she screwed the cap back on, she turned to Tate.

"You said when you aren't out on the rodeo circuit, you ranch. Where do you live?"

"South of Kennewick." The ranch his grandfather started back in the early 1900s and his father made successful through unwavering dedication and plain old hard work had always been his home. "If you head toward Umatilla and take the last exit before you cross into Oregon, we're about ten miles off the beaten path on the Washington side of the border."

"I've never driven around much in that area." In the time she'd been in the Tri-Cities, Kenzie hadn't done any exploring. She was rarely home long enough to do more than catch up on laundry and visit her one close friend.

"Are you originally from the Tri-Cities?" Tate asked, wondering where Kenzie grew up. She seemed like the very persona of a fashionable city girl, opposite of the type of girl he thought would someday fit into his lifestyle.

"No, my family lives in Portland." Kenzie brushed imaginary lint from her skirt. She knew the next question Tate would ask and beat him to it. "I moved to Kennewick three years ago because I needed to get out of Portland. My best friend lives near Pendleton and encouraged me to move closer. I chose the Tri-Cities area because it works well with my job. I spend a lot of time traveling and being close to an airport is essential."

"What made you want to leave Portland?" Tate stretched his legs beneath the seat in front of him. He hated flying, not because he was afraid of the plane crashing, but mostly because he felt cramped and uncomfortable the entire time. Whoever designed the seats must not have taken long legs and broad shoulders into account.

"Let's just say the city wasn't quite big enough to keep from running into my former fiancé and his very pregnant girlfriend." A flash of anger fired in her eyes.

At Tate's raised eyebrow, she shook her head. "It really was for the best. We were at the bakery, doing a cake tasting for our wedding, when a woman ran in and started screaming at Sonny, slapping his face. Apparently, she'd just found out she was pregnant. She demanded he tell me the truth, and he confessed he'd been seeing her on the side."

"More than seeing her, I'd say." Indignant on behalf of the woman he'd just met, he thought her ex-fiancé had to be a certified idiot to mess up a future with Kenzie. However, if the man hadn't been an idiot, Tate wouldn't be sitting across from her, enjoying their conversation and hoping he'd see her again.

"Anyway, I ran into them all the time. Since my job isn't based in a specific area, it doesn't really matter where I live. When Megan called and invited me to stay with her for a while, I decided to take her up on the offer. The drive from Helix to the airport in Pasco grew old in a hurry, so I rented an apartment in Kennewick." Uneasy, she glanced at Tate. "Now you know more about me than you ever wanted to."

"Hardly." He wondered if her skin would feel as soft as it looked as he studied her strong cheekbones and creamy complexion. Popping his knuckles seemed the only way to keep from reaching across the aisle and indulging his curiosity by touching her cheek. When Kenzie cringed at the sound, he stopped and gripped the armrest. "Your friend Megan — is she, by any chance, Megan Montgomery?"

"Yes. Do you know her?" Kenzie's voice carried a note of friendly interest.

"Yep. I know her husband, Owen. He purchases cattle from us and we've bought horses from them for years." Tate was surprised he and Kenzie hadn't run into each other before, since the Montgomery clan liked to entertain and often hosted barbecues and dinners. "Megan's fed us more than a time or two."

"Wow. I'll have to tell Megan I met you." She made a mental note to call her friend later that evening. "When you say us and we, who else lives on the ranch with you?"

Tate laughed and the sound resonated somewhere deep and untouched inside Kenzie, drawing out her smile.

"It's just me. Well, me and my foreman, Monte, and the ranch hands. My dad moved into an assisted living facility in Richland about a month ago, so I'm still getting used to rattling around the house by myself when I'm home."

"Oh, I'm sorry. Is your father unwell?" Kenzie asked, wondering what type of ailment required Tate's father to move into a care home.

"Nothing is wrong with Pop except old age. He turned ninety on his last birthday and finally agreed it was time for him to retire," Tate said, chuckling. He loved to see the reaction on people's faces when he told them his father's age.

Determined to be a bachelor his whole life, Tate's father, Kent, didn't know what hit him when he met a beautiful young woman who turned his world upside down.

"I can see by the look on your face, you're trying to do the math and coming up shy a few years," Tate teased with a knowing grin. "I'm twenty-nine. Pop was nearly sixty when he married my mama. She was in her late twenties. Most folks thought it was quite a scandal for them to get married, but they loved each other. I don't think Pop ever recovered from losing Mama. I was about eleven when she had kidney failure and died. We all thought she was in good health, but it seemed to hit her out of the blue. It's been just me and Pop since. He's done remarkably well for his age, but the winter was hard on him and he was ready to move off the ranch and into town once spring arrived. He's in great shape, but I still worry about leaving him home alone. He agreed assisted living was a good option."

"I'm sorry, Tate. I know how hard it is to lose a parent," Kenzie said, not wanting to bare her soul to this stranger. "Do you have any siblings?"

"Nope, but I've got a bunch of friends who are as close as brothers and some cousins, however many times removed, who live a few hours away in Grass Valley." He smiled as they made small talk the rest of the trip.

When the pilot announced the plane would

soon land, they both glanced at their watches. They'd made up most of the lost time.

"I've enjoyed this flight more than any I have in a long time, Kenzie. Thank you for talking with me," Tate said as they landed and gathered their things in anticipation of leaving the plane.

"It was nice to visit with you, Tate. I hope you do well at the rodeo." She genuinely wanted him to win. It was hard to remain cool and aloof around such a warm, inviting personality.

Despite the alarms sounding in her head to stay far away from him, Kenzie was grateful she had the opportunity to meet the charming cowboy.

"I do, too. It's a long way to go to not at least place," Tate said with the grin Kenzie was starting to think of as his trademark.

Some irrational part of her wanted to kiss each dimple in his scruffy cheeks.

Together they hurried through the airport. When they arrived at the point where they would go their separate ways, Tate shifted his bag and placed his free hand on Kenzie's arm, pulling her to a stop. Gently taking her hand in his, he smiled, trying to ignore the powerful force surging from their joined fingers up his arm.

"I hope we run into each other again." He sincerely hoped he would see the beautiful girl another time. Although he'd just met her, he knew she would linger in his thoughts.

"That would be nice." Suddenly, she felt very shy. "You never know when we'll meet at the airport."

"Sure don't, since we both seem to travel

frequently." Tate raised an eyebrow at Kenzie, giving her a beseeching look while shrugging his broad shoulders. "Wish me luck?"

"Of course." She smiled and squeezed the hand he still held. Thoughts of how nice his palm fit against hers infiltrated her resolve to walk away and not give Tate another thought. "Good luck."

"I meant a good luck kiss." The smile he bestowed on her had charmed many women into doing his will.

"Oh, I… um…" With a slim likelihood of seeing the handsome rodeo star again, Kenzie desperately wanted to kiss him. Before she could talk herself out of doing something crazy and completely out of character, she placed a warm, moist kiss to Tate's enticing mouth then stepped back. Her lips sizzled from the brief contact.

"Ride 'em, cowboy." Flushed, her cheeks burned as she turned and started walking away from temptation dressed in a cowboy hat and snug-fitting jeans.

"Kenzie!" Tate called after her, stunned by the impact of the kiss.

When she stopped and looked over her shoulder, he shot her a teasing grin. "Make them all dewy-eyed, Miss Dewdrop."

Kenzie laughed and waved before racing toward baggage claim. Nearly running through the airport, she caught a taxi and made it to her meeting with five minutes to spare.

Available on Amazon

Hopeless romantic Shanna Hatfield spent ten years as a newspaper journalist before moving into the field of marketing and public relations. Sharing the romantic stories she dreams up in her head is a perfect outlet for her love of writing, reading, and creativity. She and her husband, lovingly referred to as Captain Cavedweller, reside in the Pacific Northwest.

Shanna loves to hear from readers. Connect with her online:
Blog: shannahatfield.com
Facebook: Shanna Hatfield's Page
Shanna Hatfield's Hopeless Romantics Group
Pinterest: Shanna Hatfield
Email: shanna@shannahatfield.com

Made in the USA
Columbia, SC
14 December 2021

51409881R00115